MANAGING GLOBAL SURVIVAL

To Elliott & Marlene —

with friendship and appreciation

Dan

MANAGING GLOBAL SURVIVAL

an intriguing possibility

Don Lebell, PhD

iUniverse, Inc.

New York Lincoln Shanghai

Managing Global Survival
an intriguing possibility

iUniverse books may be ordered through booksellers or by
contacting:

iUniverse
2021 Pine Lake Road, Suite 100
Lincoln, NE 68512
www.iuniverse.com
1-800-Authors (1-800-288-4677)

Certain cited organizations exist. Certain events portrayed did
take place. However this is a work of fiction. All of the other
organizations and events as well as places, incidents and dialogue
in this novel are either products of the author's imagination or are
used fictitiously.

ISBN: 978-0-595-43218-9 (pbk)
ISBN: 978-0-595-87559-7 (ebk)

Printed in the United States of America

To Jane and our respective progeny,
for helping me to love, understand, and communicate with
Earthlings.

Acknowledgments

This is to acknowledge the several patient friends, relatives, and colleagues who reviewed this book's early drafts. Plagiarizing their best insights has enriched this work; their criticisms I've forgiven and moved on.

Special thanks are due to my editor Janet Rothman, for her grudging acceptance of my sometimes grandiose vocabulary and rambling sentences. This provocative style, I argued, would sharpen the reader's critical mindset in confronting the themes presented. While pleading for coherency, Janet also contributed substantive ideas for which I am grateful.

Finally I wish to acknowledge the intrepid reader, diligently seeking wisdom and enlightenment, undeterred by lengthy monologues and turgid prose—impediments without which a broader readership might develop, necessitating a second printing, book tours, TV appearances, a stretch limo, dinner at the White House. I'd hate all that.

Actually, with more candor than levity, I felt the issues raised are too urgent for delay merely to enhance the book's readability. However, the reader's comfort has not been totally disregarded in that the book is organized as short segments with minimal continuity. This modular format should facilitate snacking and convenience breaks.

Preface

At parties, I would comment to my dinner partner that the sky was falling. As a systems engineer, it was obvious to me how and why our world was becoming unstable, and the dire consequences if we failed to apply the basic principles and best practices of management and systems engineering. I would explain that having consulted for a diversity of clients, exposure to their quaint cultures and behaviors had imparted unique insights, which I'd be willing to share over coffee and dessert.

With fewer dinner invitations, I considered writing a book on the subject. Maybe I'd write it as if through the eyes of an extraterrestrial—not much stretch for a nomadic consultant accustomed to sudden immersion in exotic places. An ET's perspective could convey cultural objectivity and invite the reader to "think outside the box" while assessing the underlying themes.

Ah, but might this ET format offend readers just looking for experiential insights from a no-nonsense management/engineering consultant, without a lot of fictionalized clutter? Conversely, those readers interested only in a sci-fi narrative probably wouldn't want insights and wisdom disrupting the story's gripping moments. Well as Joan of Arc must have observed, you can't please everyone.

So what would be the underlying themes?

• Proliferation of weapons, technologies, telecommunication, and drugs has preceded mass education, enlightened leadership, and responsive institutions. That's not good.

• Solutions are available along with the requisite resources. That's good.

• Perspectives and tools of engineering and management could help. Also good.

• The same perspectives and tools can apply not just to global survival, but to a wide range of business and personal involvements as well. That's good, too—particularly for readers not especially interested in global survival.

But aside from bits of humor, sex, and violence to stimulate book sales, this management book's quite serious purpose would be to encourage systematic identification and consideration of the important issues and alternatives.

Hmm … and that would be a book about managing? Absolutely, because if the issues and alternatives are understood, managing becomes easy—or at least plausible. So behind this book's verbiage would lurk valuable suggestions for managing global survival or whatever else needed managing. What sort of valuable suggestions?

• Intuition can be augmented by simply sketching your situation as a system surrounded by its environment and key stakeholders. Diagram the system itself as a rudimentary anatomy chart via functional boxes and connecting arrows. Even such an elementary portrayal can frequently illuminate paradoxes, imminent catastrophes, or new opportunities. Such charts are also useful for opening presentations, such as a detailed computer study for the anal retentive.

- The important bottlenecks and openings are often not where we expect them. Ask yourself why world hunger persists, why your schedule is always overloaded, why the nuclear proliferation threat keeps getting worse, or why your primary relationship is great but not quite as great as it could be. A stakeholders-system diagram could highlight crucial bottlenecks, each one tagged with roadmapped remedies, color-coded, if you have enough crayons. Even at this rudimentary level of detail, your perception and judgment may become more focused, informed, or enlightened.

- Reality denial is popular, especially for ominous trends or the nasty details of how things actually work. Accepting such realities can spoil your day. But admitting and then acting on them might save your company.

- Ostentatiously prevailing over opposition, undeterred by the details or uncertainties, that's always invigorating. Such focus and tenacity will be applauded, especially by your bankruptcy attorney.

- Planning is exhilarating and fun. Communicating and winning acceptance for the plan is not. Implementing the plan is often obnoxious hard work. If you can't delegate it, at least request your management's unwavering endorsement of the steps ahead, as well as commitment to the necessary resources and schedule, responsibilities, and incentives. Such requests, seldom granted, will at least demonstrate your understanding of gestures; helpful towards a promotion to management

- Don't waste time and energy grieving over failed initiatives. If it had been easy, it would have already been done. On the other hand, don't let success breed complacency, organizational arthritis, or undue reverence for obsolete strategies. Since this advice is difficult to follow consistently, it's always prudent to retain a highly visible, disposable deputy.

At first glance these ideas seem no more than intuition or common-sense clichés that we all know. However such clichés have at times been ignored with regret by some very smart people. Moreover, it doesn't hurt to review an immutable truth now and then.

So thinking about all this, pondering whether to write a book, for distraction I decided to install my new voice-recognition software, whereupon ...

Introduction

Testing ... testing ... yeah, it works—finally! No more 1-800 calls to Bangladesh ... at least not today. Now let's see how the voice synthesizer recites my incoming e-mail ... and here it comes ...

Hmm, good intonation with the baritone voice, no lengthy pauses, spam-blocker working. This is great! I can have a beer and watch the game while listening.

Excuse me sir, may I ask you a few interview questions?

What? Whoa, absolutely not! How did you get in? How did you get past my spam filter? I designed an impenetrable firewall configuration. Tell me. I really need to know.

Certainly, sir, and I apologize for the intrusion. My planet's technology for penetrating filters is highly advanced. I suppose it derives from our recognition of the importance of transparency in all facets of—sorry, I'm always a bit garrulous after a long journey. I already know you're a systems engineer, so you'll be able to give me crisp, orderly responses. This won't take long. So may we proceed?

Sure, at least until I can see how you got past my firewall. I'm running a test while we talk. What are you selling? What's the pitch?

No sir, you don't understand. I really just need some information.

Right. OK, you're not sounding like the usual huckster wanting to shrink or expand some part of my body or net worth. Tell me what this is about. Then I'll decide whether to be interviewed.

Thank you, sir. I don't want to extend this any more than you do. Actually I'm here in part because my previous report was considered disrespectful of Earthlings. Disrespect is another very important taboo on my planet. As a systems engineer, you, of course, would know that transparency and respect for others are among the preconditions for stability—again I'm digressing. Sorry.

Hey, you sound almost authentic. So OK, but what are you really? Are you a student? A pollster? A politician? Some of ours could be from your neighborhood, come to think of it.

No, I'm what you'd probably call a cleaner.

Huh? So, what do you clean?

It's not just cleaning. I'm responsible for the analysis, followed by debris cleanup after your planet implodes.

OK, now I get it. You're selling seats on the next spacecraft or post-Armageddon freezer slots, or some insurance gimmick. Which is it?

No, it's nothing like that.

Look, I know this is a put-on. Do I want to e-mail with a cosmic janitor? I'm afraid I'd feel a little silly.

With all due respect, sir, you already sound a little silly. I'll try switching my voice synthesizer setting from falsetto to basso. That might impart a more substantial tone to your pronouncements, irrespective of content. And I don't mind you treating this as a joke or role playing, just so long as I get the information I need.

That's very magnanimous of you. OK, let's give it a try. Mr. Cleaner, I am deeply honored by your visit. From the vantage point of your highly advanced civilization, what advice can you impart to us oh-so-primitive Earthlings in order to avoid Armageddon?

Well, just from this first encounter, I'd suggest that you Earthlings should be more open to unexpected ideas and opportunities, even if seemingly from outer space.

OK fellow, you've got your interview, but I can't right now. Same time tomorrow?

Excellent! I look forward to it.

Session 1

May we start the interview? Rather than e-mail, I've taken the liberty of setting up a more private, interactive chat room for us. I've signed on as ET.

Good idea, ET. OK, I'm signed up too, as SysEng. Now let me interview you a bit first. I always like to know something about who I'm talking with. And actually I'd like you to talk a bit so I can adjust my new voice synthesizer.

Yes of course. Please proceed.

Now, in your vast experience, Mr. ET, what causes planets like Earth to "implode?"

Lots of reasons. With young planets, it can be some physical or biological catastrophe; a seismic or volcanic event, or a cross-species pandemic—that sort of thing. With more mature planets that support evolution of relatively advanced civilizations like yours, everything becomes increasingly fragile, and you don't need a cataclysm to destabilize things. You must understand that it's very rare and precarious in nature for any planet to sustain a civilization—even one at your stage. No offense, but the slightest nudge can destabilize it.

1

Like what?

For example, your planet's spin axis isn't quite perpendicular to the plane of the earth's orbit around your sun. As an engineer, you might see that little spin axis deviation from the vertical as a minor design imperfection. But that little imperfection causes your four seasons, which in turn cause flora and fauna to evolve adaptively. Birds migrate, and humans collaborate to prepare for surviving winter. That, in turn, prepares them for anticipating and surviving a wider range of threats during their lifetimes. Without that little deviation of the spin axis, you'd have evolved only sedentary species, vulnerable to any little triviality, like a volcano or a small climate fluctuation. In my line of work, I see that quite often.

So is your cleanup report anticipating that sort of eventuality? Do you see our spin axis inclination shifting over the eons or some such cataclysm? Come on, give me a break.

No. Actually, we see a rather unusual situation at hand, the intensifying confluence of technology shocks but in juxtaposition with sociopolitical infrastructures already saturated from population and environmental overload together with—

Uh, what are you talking about?

Sorry. Let's see if I can simplify it for you. The primitive men of your civilization who survived and procreated were those who were most proficient in the more advanced technologies of hunting, gathering, and fighting. Correspondingly, the women who survived and procreated were those most proficient in the more advanced technologies of gang-rape avoidance and child-bearing. Then came your discoveries of fire, the wheel, tools, and weapons. These technologies, while extending longevity, gradually revolutionized tribal behaviors; agriculture, family formation, and clustering of tribes with primitive modes of barter, religion, and combat.

Yes, I know all that. So what?

Then came the technologies of materials and energy acquisition, processing and distribution, powering your industrial revolution, imposing requirements for training, organizational development, management, and wealth redistribution.

So what's your point?

My point is that each technology replaced scarcity with abundance of something; disrupting and forcing realignments of the economic, sociopolitical, and cultural fabric of your so-called civilization. Introduction of these technologies was tolerable and not destabilizing when they occurred singularly, locally, or gradually, hence in digestible sequences; that is, they did not tear up the socioeconomic status quo more than necessary.

And therefore?

Don't you see? Your planet is presently grappling with the sudden and concurrent onset of powerful new technologies, shocks that simultaneously provide for mass dissemination of potent weapons, potent labor disruptions, and instant mass communication. But these jolting advances have not been preceded by mass education or exposure to mitigating mechanisms to facilitate socioeconomic mobility, safeguard the middle class, human rights, and a welfare safety net. These missing components are essential to a functional democracy. So you have an indigestible overload, hence implosion!

Do all you extraterrestrials speak so pretentiously?

Sorry. It's just that we automatically adapt to the proximate speaker's vocabulary and style.

Touché. OK, what's next? What else is on your mind?

What's on my mind right now is that when you hear from an educated, objective source that your little world is about to disintegrate, you might at least want to give it some thought.

OK, I'm thinking. I'm thinking that you probably mean "explosion" rather than "implosion," or am I being picky?

Yes, "picky" sounds right. By implosion I refer to the collapse of your civilization, not explosion of the physical world.

But you just demonstrated in your tiresome lecture that we've had innumerable technology shocks and our societies haven't imploded. In fact, they have always become even more robust. Today, globalization is producing economies of scale and distribution, unending technology advances, information access, military capabilities of unprecedented kind and quantity, entertainment, and education. Why, our prosperity, its accessibility, and durability have never been greater!

Well, apparently I'm not the only one from a distant planet here.

I suppose that's your intergalactic sarcasm? How can you even suggest that our democracy isn't functional? Our democracy works just fine, thank you very much. It has served us virtually unchanged for 230 years and we successfully export it around the world with great results ultimately, if not at first.

Frankly, your Armageddon scenario isn't very persuasive even though you sound like what I'd expect an extraterrestrial to sound like. Look, there are always complainers who get attention from journalists who are constantly searching for conflicts to report. This planet is nowhere near the brink of extinction! You've been taken in, my friend. You're supposed to be from a more advanced civilization. You should get out more and find some fresh perspectives!

Hello? Are you still there? Have I insulted your tender sensitivities? Are you totally preoccupied with your Armageddon scenario?

No. At the moment I'm totally preoccupied wondering whether on this planet it's more ludicrous to be anachronistic or myopic.

OK, that's it. It's third quarter with Dallas 1st and 10 on the 15 and I don't need your—hey, what happened to my cable feed? Did you do that? Are you really from outer space? Get Dallas back! Ah, there it is.

So why don't you go get some fresh air and ideas while I find out how well our passing attack is working?

That's a very good suggestion. Same time tomorrow?

I'd said one interview ... OK; I'm willing to give you another try but no more insults. Got it?

Yes. Excellent.

Session 2

Hello. Hello. ET, are you there?

Yes, of course.

Good. I've turned off my voice-synthesizer. That way I can skim or study your text messages at my own pace. Go ahead, I'm ready for you.

Fine. Following your suggestion, I've been looking around to augment what I'd been able to learn at home. And I find it all rather amazing. I appreciate your having made that suggestion.

Of course. You seemed bright, so I was pretty sure that exposure to a bit of reality would straighten out some of your naïve ideas. Tell me what you've learned.

Certainly. But first, would you tell me something of your personal background?

Well I'm a 47-year-old engineer, recently divorced with a son and a daughter, both in college. As a freelance management consultant, my systems engineering background gives me somewhat unique perspectives and tools helpful to my clients. I ski, sail, play tennis, work out, argue with my kids, and enjoy smart, sexy women, so long as they don't talk too much or want "a meaningful relationship." Why do you ask?

It helps me to better understand your comments. For example, your initial reaction to me would be considered patronizing and arrogant on my planet. But here, it may just be the culture or how humans react to a new idea.

What have I been learning? For starters, thanks to the mass media telecommunications you've enthused over, today you've got 80 percent of the planet suddenly discovering that the other 20 percent have most of the food, jobs, shelter, health care, property, and disdain for the 80 percent. And except for a few idealistic but outnumbered humanitarians, the 20 percent don't really want to share those things, or even the opportunities to acquire them.

Wrong! We have many programs and institutions devoted to third-world development. And the numbers I look at suggest favorable trends in third-world literacy, longevity, and health care. That's despite the recipients' truculence, ingratitude, indolence, and disrespect for their own laws and community. Look, I've been there and seen it all. Just last year on my cruise-ship vacation—I know what I'm talking about. Oh, and I apologize if I sounded patronizing and arrogant.

Well, you certainly know Earthlings better than I do. On my planet, we encourage entrepreneurs, but our smartest ones don't grasp at opportunities until they see others making it work for them. Caution often appears as apathy. And typically those who do advance a bit are initially more angry than grateful as they begin to see the wealth disparities more clearly. And of course, they are feeling stressed.

Why stressed? Shouldn't they be just a tad euphoric?

Possibly so. I don't know how it is here on Earth. But on my planet, small socioeconomic advances engender guilt about those left behind, or fear of becoming a more prominent target or of failing to adapt. These fears are intensified simply by being with unfamiliar people in unfamiliar surroundings which often dilutes one's sense of self. It's what we call "ambiguity of place."

Ambiguity of place? That must be something unique to your planet.

I don't believe so. Here's a simpler example: In raising a family, we must deal with the middle child's ambiguity of place. Since middle children are not inherently distinctive in the family structure, they require special attention. When middle children try to win approval by emulating the oldest or the youngest, the applause they seek is muted at best, often inducing passive withdrawal or aggressive adventurism.

OK, yes, we have that on Earth, too. Now that you mention it, the same thing happens not only in families, but in our other hierarchical organizations as well. High-level executives and entry-level workers readily accept their respective places. Any tensions and conflicts relate to external issues of their work, job security, and compensation. But middle managers and more senior workers often have insecurity or identity issues with their image, ego, and status.

I see it frequently in firms of lawyers and doctors. Wherever organizational dissonance or high turnover rates occur, it usually comes from the "almost equal" personnel. Likewise, studies would probably find that instigators of urban riots and most wars have been the almost-equals. So I suppose you are saying that populations which first experience some modest socioeconomic progress may not express gratitude to those who helped or made room for them?

That's right. In any case, right here, right now, increasing segments of your 80 percent have leaders with serious weapons, ano-

nymity, mobility, rage, and conviction. And while most of the 80 percent are too ill, hungry, or depleted from work or parenting to get involved, a small but growing percentage are becoming active under increasingly sophisticated leaders.

Some of what you say may be true for the moment and I grant there are pockets of ignorance and poverty quite resistant to our demonstrably superior system of equitable political and socioeconomic opportunities. But most of these people are just too backward in their values, culture, and education to "get it" and move forward, to help each other in community development within the law. Look, I live in the most powerful, dynamic, democratic, and generous country in the world, qualities directly resulting from some of your "powerless" folks figuring things out and moving up, helping themselves and their country. The upward-mobility paths are there, well-traveled in the past and conspicuously available for the future.

That's very helpful. I am new here and have much to learn.

I understand. What else can I clarify for you?

Well, forgive me if this sounds argumentative. But I still don't quite understand how your "upward mobility" works. In particular, I get the impression that when new science and technologies are developed, they are most often owned by the entities already endowed with the best current Science and Technology. When interest and dividends are paid on capital, payment goes to those who already own the preponderance of capital. Your voters, when conferring political power, make their choices from information provided by those already holding the political power. When justice is administered, those previously favored by the justice system and its administrators are again most favored. Quality education is predominantly available to students from the most educated classes. Globalization of labor supply and demand, plus new labor-substi-

tution technologies, weakens labor's traditional ways of accessing economic and sociopolitical power. And finally, when the military power that supports it all is increasingly concentrated in the hands of those already possessing the greatest military power, your upward-mobility path would seem tenuous at best.

Well, as you say, you're new here. The status quo is favored a bit, of course. That's how any system retains the stability essential to fulfilling its purpose. And incidentally, on this planet, "survival of the fittest" works for us humans as well as for other species. So if you look further, you'll see that the opportunities are really there.

And I recommend that you use your eyes and ears more than your mouth until you begin to get a clue about America. Check out how this country was formed from impoverished, outnumbered, dedicated fighters seeking freedom and social justice.

As a matter of fact, I have done a bit of homework and do understand and respect that chapter of American history. Even aside from combat accomplishments, to have designed and installed a government structure, unique in its protection of citizens, yet able to function effectively at the national level as well—truly remarkable! I would mention, however, that you had some important advantages not available today.

I know I'm going to regret asking, but … like what?

You had protective oceans against invaders. You had contemporaneous wars in Europe which spilled over in ways helpful to the colonists, thanks in part to some fortuitous or gifted diplomacy there. You had recognition of the common threat, such that "hanging together or hanging separately" was a meaningful slogan. You had no concentrated natural endowments—such as oil, diamond deposits, or a solitary river—endowments whose very concentration fosters corrupt, totalitarian autocracies. You had a citizenry accus-

tomed to deferred gratification and community collaboration, thanks to harsh winters, marauding natives and animals, yet whose 16th century muskets could not level a building or destroy a city. And you had an amazingly few gifted, educated, and astute leaders whose affluence, coupled with grass-roots proximity, provided them the perspectives to develop a government protective of property, citizen rights, and national security—truly amazing.

My compliments! You've got it right. So why all the negativity?

It's simply that "hanging together or hanging separately" is the only one of these advantages that seems to have endured.

Ouch! Look, if you are so concerned about our planet's survival being jeopardized by third-world deprivations, why didn't you—correction: why *don't* you go visit one of those countries instead of ours? I'm starting to like that idea a lot.

To answer your question, it appeared that America by word and deed has recently been intensifying and accelerating your planet's destabilization. Partly, I'm here to understand the underlying forces and whether their reversal is possible. Also, I'd been led to believe that Americans are affluent, powerful, and enjoy a tradition of selflessly helping those who are less-fortunate.

I wanted to see first-hand why that no longer seems to be working. Your attitude is helping me begin to understand. I now see that there are important things I've yet to learn.

Really? Aren't all you ETs omniscient? Don't answer, please. I need a break. Tomorrow, same time?

Agreed, and thanks. I'm learning a lot from you.

Session 3

You said there were important things you still needed to learn about us. Like what?

Well, for example, there is the apparent importance of organized religions in your existential struggle. Is that some remnant from your caveman days?

Certainly not! Don't religions play a dominant role on your oh-so-advanced planet?

They did, but we got over it. Our earlier organized religions provided powerful psychic rewards: approval from a paternalistic higher authority, exoneration from inadequacy-inspired guilt, and hence from responsibilities which are beyond fulfillment. They conferred instant self-esteem, and membership in a community. Our religions even designated certain cities, shrines, and other real estate parcels as god-given for the true believers—all of which facilitated the members' docility and support of their organizations.

Off-hand, such benefits wouldn't seem potent enough for long-term growth and stability of those religious movements. How did the organizations retain power?

Well, there was also the certification and sanctification of births, marriages, deaths, and property rights. Those sorts of things were reserved for the scrupulously observant; a very powerful strategy in maintaining allegiance.

Even so …

And there were always external enemies designated as evil, to be feared, loathed, and expunged, following which, life—or after-life would be, well, heavenly for those members in good-standing. Moreover, in order to kill enemies enthusiastically, warriors needed to feel righteous and fearless. Religion, especially with the promise of an attractive after-life, provided these elements, hence a decisive combat edge over the secular warrior. It's almost embarrassing to recall such a primitive stage of our civilization.

Hmm. You seem quite knowledgeable and logical. I'm guessing your specialty must be astrophysics, mathematics, history, or some combination? Maybe you'll tell me later.

Yes, later. As I describe our ancient religions, I'm wondering if there are any similarities to your religions here and now. I assume, of course, that you've stopped genital mutilations and fighting over which deity is most authentic. If not, I can assure you, there are less-barbaric ways to get people's attention in order to program their values, beliefs, and behavior for the common good.

Well, I'd say that we've made some progress; we don't sacrifice virgins anymore. How did your planet become secular? Sometimes I wish our culture—it might be much easier to do systems engineering.

As I understand it, our poor people were quite religious, attracted for the psychic rewards I've mentioned. Our affluent people were also religious, perhaps for community solidarity and as justification for their self-indulgences. Also, in those early times, imminent death was greatly feared, drawing parishioners to com-

forting beliefs in immortality, familial and tribal continuity, the hereafter, that sort of thing—and of course, they had the time and resources. As I say, it's a bit embarrassing to even discuss it, and I'm no expert in the field.

What about your middle class?

I'd guess that they were just too busy doing the necessary work. Unshielded from their reality in order to do that work, the good and bad consequences of their own actions dominated attention and didn't require mystical explanations or justifications. Also, the middle class must have lacked the time, psychological hunger, and discretionary resources for taking religion very seriously. They had to settle for faith in themselves rather than something more exotic. Then from enlightened self-interest they gradually bonded with the rich and assimilated the poor. Mostly secular, their influence on the more stringently religious rich and poor extremes must have gradually prevailed.

Do you see our civilization eventually moving in that secular direction? At present, we Earthlings seem to be increasingly devoted to organized religion, in contrast to what happened on your planet. Might that not help us in the long run?

What long run? Look, you provide mass communication without education. The affluent class is easily portrayed by the media as uncaring, even contemptuous, malevolent, and exploitative. Stir in guns, and unregulated revenue from the drug, sex, and oil industries, and you have very fertile soil for militant religious fervor to flourish, certainly within poor communities. If your religious leaders aren't already responding to this growth market, charismatic entrepreneurs will quickly supplant your traditional leadership, repackage the product, and meet the opportunities presented.

It's a shame. This was a nice little planet, but the time sequencing of your technology shocks—think how it might have been if mass education and socioeconomic development had preceded mass dissemination of weapons here. Don't feel bad; it probably happens this way with lots of little planets.

Well, aren't you the cheery one? Is there no hope?

Probably not. Once in a while something peculiar happens and a planet makes it. Mine did, although I'm not exactly sure how. That's not my field.

Not your field? Then what is your field? And why did you select me?

Please, one question at a time. I'm still getting used to your strange language. OK, I'm a musicologist.

A musicologist? You're kidding. Check your thesaurus; it's a mistake. Why in the world would they send—sorry, let me rephrase that. I don't mean to sound rude, but on this planet we'd never use musicologists for such work.

I understand your incredulity. Almost the first thing I did upon arrival was to seek out colleagues here; the two musicologists I found are also "cleaners," but they clean office floors, windows, and restrooms. Since my supervisor is a poet, I also checked on how your poets are utilized here. She won't be amused by my report.

Again, I have to ask: why would they send a musicologist? Did they send you here as punishment for some crime—or maybe as a joke?

I'm not sure I can explain it to you. Everything is so primitive here, but I'll try. At home, we place great value on aesthetics and self-expression unfettered by context. Those who are capable of bridging the gap to structure and functionalism, especially poets and musicologists, are not only respected, but are assigned to our most challenging societal concerns. A more interesting question to me is why I was advised to contact a systems engineer such as yourself rather than a real manager ... no offense intended.

Look, I'm still not convinced you are what you claim, but your portrayal of the planet's precarious state, well … it's almost persuasive. And since I've never worked with an extraterrestrial—or a musicologist, for that matter—I'd be willing to continue this Internet chat-room conversation a bit further. If your prediction is correct, collaborating to save our planet would obviously be worth the effort to me. And aside from satisfying your intellectual curiosity, wouldn't you also like to reduce your cleanup work?

Actually, it would be sort of interesting to see if we could at least hypothesize a strategic plan and roadmap together, irrespective of whether it can be implemented. Then too, my orientation in coming here included the suggestion that when your protagonist is locked in denial, collaboration in some harmless activity such as strategic planning may help to establish trust and a more flexible posture. So yes, let's proceed.

Oh, and in my orientation, there was a suggestion about climate-setting and closure. So how did Dallas do?

Badly, but thanks for asking. The best part of the second half was watching the cheerleaders.

What? Isn't football played with just two teams of eleven?

Never mind. Let's move on. Tomorrow at 6 PM?

Fine.

SESSION 4

I know this is just a role-playing exercise, but I admit to being caught up in it and I've been thinking about it quite a bit. So I'm inclined to proceed with the same sort of methodology I use in my work and personal decision-making as well.

Good. Tell me more of what you do in your work. I'm sure we can use it in our collaboration.

OK, but first, just as you wanted to understand my background a bit, I'd like to understand yours. Do you look like Earthlings? Do you live in a city? Do you have brothers and sisters?

We look virtually identical to Earthlings. I live in a high-rise building in our largest city. I have no siblings that I know of. Why do you ask?

Even with our chat room's instant messaging, it's hard to know how well the communicating is going, without context or body language confirmation. That's why I ask.

Is that all?

Not quite. I'm not sure I'd answer you face-to-face but, well, last night, I had the most erotic dream that I can remember. It started with our chat room dialogue just like now. But then suddenly, we were walking on the beach hand-in-hand, and you had become female, your sister I'd guess. And then back at my apartment; well … let's just move on. Do you have such dreams?

Never until very recently. Strange that you ask. I think I'd better take some of your air samples home for analysis. And I should leave soon anyway. Strange …

Please don't even think about leaving for a while. Tell me more about your background.

Since you know so little about my planet, well … my background out of context can't make much sense to you, but let's try. I'm single, 38 in Earth years, a professional musicologist and composer. I've not married nor have I had adult physical relationships as you have.

What? Why not? Do they put something in your food?

That's funny! No, our advanced sensory implant is self-controlled, and stimulates the brain with whatever sensory experiences are needed or desired. And we cultivate self-esteem, sense of identity, security, and emotional development early within the nuclear family. The urge to procreate directly, as performed by the lower species, is permitted, but considered perverted and backward since the State manages it all scientifically with computer-controlled sperm and egg banks.

Our time, energy, and interests are preserved for self-development and service to career, family, and community. Those wanting to start families simply provide detailed specifications for preferred offspring characteristics. Trust me; it is entirely tranquil and fulfilling. The few times I've personally started into relationships, they've always felt cumbersome, contrived, and demeaning, and certainly not exciting. So I quickly exited.

Tell me about it!

I am. Oh, that's one of your colloquialisms.

So when I have felt the desire to procreate, I've simply donated to the sperm/egg bank. As you know, I have no experience with science or management, but in other fields I've had a strong interest in education and I compete rather well in athletics. Somehow I've not felt the urge to have my own family—maybe when I've learned more of life. So please help me learn, Mr. Engineer.

A microchip implanted sex toy? Wow!

OK, as a management and engineering systems practitioner, I urge an orderly approach to problem delineation and resolution. By that I mean that one should first be clear on the situation. For example let's accept your previous notion that my planet's civilization has become an unstable system headed toward oblivion. That would be our "situation".

Next we need to be clear on our purpose which is to devise plausible initiatives, maybe even a roadmap for stabilizing my planet by adopting the stabilizing attributes of your planet. System requirements can then be devised and specified. We next design initiatives and their implementation roadmaps for testing or for scenario analysis of various outcomes.

Aren't these the same functions that your architects perform for a building project?

Hey, that's very good, Mr. ET. Yes, and we use that term "systems architecture" accordingly, whether the system is a building or any other kind of system. From there we simply embark on the management processes: win consensus, decide on the program initiatives, and assign responsibilities. Next we implement the acquisition and processing of resources and information, via programs controlled with forecasting and decision processing for implementation.

Good grief, you really are a systems engineer!
Yes, thank you.

Incidentally you were wondering why, since Earth's problems manifest as "management failures," you were led to a systems engineer rather than a manager. Managers manage organizations which are actually systems. Prior to operation of the system-organization, entrepreneurs will have designed and launched the organization, even detected and corrected the inevitable early mistakes. Some entrepreneurs are analytic and systematic, and will proceed with the same sort of orderly steps I've recited above. Others will rely more on intuition, and will let these steps be implicit and flexible, and without much fanfare. In any case, there's always a conceptual model; it can be implicit or explicit, whether based in past experience, a new technology, or simple intuition. And there are always start-up mistakes to be diagnosed and fixed. A colleague refers to entrepreneurs as "The Oops Brigade."

But we engineers perform those same basics functions. Managers know how to dress properly and give briefings, so they make more money. But engineers deal with systems that have volatile or ambiguous goals and roles, especially if inanimate resources are also involved. So I don't know how things are done on your planet, but it would make sense that you might come to a systems engineer rather than a manager regarding mismanagement of our planet's precarious situation.

It sounds like I'd better learn more of what you systems engineers and managers do. I don't want to suggest initiatives that you couldn't implement or understand.

Now who's sounding arrogant? OK, let me tell you a bit more about what I do as a management consultant. Hard-core systems engineering these days can be very detailed and mathematically sophisticated. We have software so powerful you wouldn't believe it. But in my experience working with complex, dynamic management problems, I've learned that often, there isn't enough data, time, client-sophistication, or even a trustworthy concept to justify using our truly classy systems software. On the other hand, rudimentary models with home-grown spreadsheets and presentation software encourage us to work at a more detailed, systematic level than is possible with intuition alone.

That's interesting. I'd say something quite similar with regard to how we work with computers in musicology. So tell me more.

Well, whether I'm planning the design for my own consulting assignment or a debate with my daughter about dropping her misanthropic boyfriend, I very briefly write out the situation, my purpose, and intention, from which I can then tailor a sketch of the system. Knowing if my intention is to analyze, design, train, plan, operate, or merely conceptualize and argue the system; that knowledge guides how much to include in my system portrayal.

I don't quite get that.

It's simple. Every system has structure, inputs and outputs, mission-goals-implementation mechanisms, strengths and weaknesses. The system's external environment contains threats, opportunities, and trends, also stakeholders with their characteristics, purposes, and intentions, their resources and infrastructures. Some of these elements I can ignore as "implicit." Others, I may need to depict in exquisite detail, all depending on my purpose. For example, if it involves decision-making or design, I'll need to add alternatives and their probable consequences.

I could go on.

Yes, evidently. What about implementation?

Good question! Even if the analysis and design has emphasized ease of implementation, it's almost always problematic. Implementation often involves structural changes, including institutional mandates, leadership, organizational design, or behavioral changes involving socioeconomic or political elements. The overall return or reward versus risk is most important, but often very subjective and complex, and perceived differently by different stakeholders. For successful change in any complex system, there needs to be an understanding and acceptance of reality, commonality of goals, and implementation commitments among the stakeholders.

It sounds challenging, to say the least.

Yes, but there are ways to make it simpler: the use of structural or anatomy charts, generic descriptors, and spreadsheets to organize all the details and data. Much of the detailed, quantitative analysis can be made routine, or is avoidable if we're careful in assessing our true purpose.

That may answer one of my questions. I've been wondering why your personal library is so limited, given the range of applications and details involved in your work.

Whoa! How do you know about my personal library? We're not using our Web cameras. Have you been in my apartment? How did you get in? How dare you!

What's the problem? I thought it would save us time in getting acquainted. For example, you have a large wall photo of the 9/11 disaster, but no family photos or clutter? You do your own oil changes for your vintage sports coupe? You use a small laptop rather than a computer console with plasma monitors? And your wardrobe ... is your sports jacket for daytime and the suit for evening? What if you spilled something? You probably never have.

For your information, I *have* spilled and in fact my other suit is at the cleaners. We don't need a big wardrobe here in Southern California. The 9/11 photo? Although it was five years ago I remember grieving not just for a friend's death but at that moment I also saw 9/11 as the end of an epoch for me, for my loved ones, my country and culture. So that photo commemorates—but wait; back to the issue. You had no business entering my apartment! I'll probably get a big bill from the security-system people responding to the break in.

What break in? You call that front door lock and security alarm a system? And you're a systems engineer?

What are you angry about? I'm the one violated here.

Violated? Nobody was violated? Is privacy that important to all you Earthlings? I can't believe it. In your immortal words, let's move on. And I admit to the mistake in not getting your permission first. Don't systems analysts and designers ever make mistakes?

Yes, of course we do. Maybe I made one, over-reacting to your "visit." You'd have no way to know that privacy is very important to us here.

Now to answer your question ... with experience, we systems people can anticipate and avoid the most frequently encountered mistakes.

What mistakes? You admit to mistakes? Where do they come from?

Mistakes derive from innumerable causes such as:

• mistaken identity of stakeholders,

• overlooking or overcommitted resources,

• inappropriate or inflexible attitudes,

- denial or myopia of the big picture, the details or imminent changes,

- a mismatch of strategy versus resources or their timing,

- misinterpreting history or system characteristics,

- ignoring common sense or seeming paradoxes,

- disregarding emerging threats and opportunities,

- misinterpreting organizational or leadership competencies, and

- misunderstanding communications or commitment.

The list is endless. Here, let me show you some others.

Thanks, maybe another time.

OK, I apologize for all the details. I don't know how else to answer your questions. The range of system applications is enormous as are our alternative modes of interaction with systems: analysis, design, operations, and more. All of which makes it mind-numbing on the first encounter. But the power, heterogeneity, and ubiquity of systems shouldn't be discouraging, especially since modern computers and software make systems increasingly accessible without much in-depth expertise.

Good comments! Right now, following your prior advice, I'm scheduled to get out and about. I'll report back Monday at our regular time. OK?

That's fine. It's Saturday night. I'd suggest a bar where you could probably stir up some action. But on second thought, with your sensory fusion chip, you probably don't need the diversion.

Session 5

So how was your weekend? This was really your first solid excursion. What have you learned?

Well, take a look. I'll e-mail you my rough notes which I'll use to prepare for reporting back home. But you're welcome to read them now. You'll see mostly a listing of surprises.

I would think so. Half of what I see on the front page of my morning newspaper seems incredible to me. So for someone from another planet ... ah, here's your download.

NOTES: Earth's size, orbit and rotation, topography, temperatures, and atmosphere match ours quite well. The flora, fauna, and people are quite similar to us in appearance. Applying my protoplasm adaptation kit seemed almost unnecessary—amazing!

But there are substantial differences. For example, Earthlings still procreate just like the other animals, which I find both repugnant and unsanitary. Their sexual tensions are intense and unremitting. I can understand how the most "enthusiastic" cave people spawned the most progeny, thereby promulgating that trait, but that was millions of Earth years ago. Yet sexual innuendo and titillation are still everywhere. It's in the advertising and product designs, and in marketing of political representatives and business leaders. Sex also seems to be the dominant control mechanism in interpersonal relationships—and how Earthlings do love to control relationships! Thank goodness we have transcended to a more enlightened state than these vulgar animals.

At home we never lie, knowing that honesty is essential to the stability of any enlightened civilization. But these Earthlings rely on dishonesty almost as a way of life. A wife pretends to enthuse over the imminent visit of her dreaded mother-in-law. A doctor exudes confident reassurances even when completely mystified by the patient's symptoms.

Beyond Earthlings' dishonest communication with each other is their confounded self-deception. Weird to encounter at first, it's probably from trying to protect and adjust the inner-self against the outer environment. If the life insurance salesman admits to himself that his product is designed to protect the insurer rather than the insured, how can he sell enthusiastically, face his family, or respect his boss—or self? If a woman admits to herself that her husband's ego is bigger than his brain and that his commitment to Monday Night Football dwarfs his commitment as a father and lover, what can she do with that insight? So all this self-deception, while perfectly understandable, is exorbitantly expensive in terms of unresolved issues and self-esteem. CONTINUED

Well, I can understand all this as your first impression, but I'm sure you'll find that we aren't that bad and … oh, here comes your second attachment.

NOTES: As I study them further, the obsessions I noted may be part of a more general orifice fetish. Earthlings seem to be quite ritualistic about all of their various openings:

The females make black marks around their eyes, perhaps to ward off evil spirits. Maybe it's some sort of raccoon worship. I can't tell. Then they insert pieces of plastic directly into or in front of their eyes. Whatever satisfaction they derive from all this must be ephemeral; they keep redoing it.

The young Earthlings insert electronic noisemakers into their ears which are loud enough to gradually destroy their auditory nerves. I can't imagine why they want to become deaf. In any case, the process induces a vacant stare, involuntary lip movements, and guttural incantations. Their bodies contort rhythmically, either in pain or to notify others that they are performing this rite and are not to be disturbed they can certainly count on my compliance.

They designate special places where groups gather for inserting nourishment. Far more effort and cost go into establishing the ambiance, arranging, and presenting the food than into producing, delivering, and preparing it for consumption! Even worse, by means of selective genetics, additives, and packaging, far more effort goes into shaping the food's eye-appeal and limiting damage from delivery or putrefaction than goes into producing the nutrient. The cost of the actual food is probably 2 percent of what the oblivious consumer pays.

I was greatly relieved to learn that their ostentatious group-intake of meticulously arranged food is not matched by similarly ritualistic defecation. In fact, it's quite the opposite. Earthlings go to great lengths to pretend that waste disposal is not even required. If unable to delay until a private moment, they will mutter something about going off to wash hands or fix make-up while the remaining stalwarts in the group conceal smirks of superiority. They also pretend to deny the existence of perspiration, nasal, and vaginal emissions—except in their flamboyant, tasteless marketing of various moisture-disposal products.

Even their protuberances that house orifices for procreation or lactation are often augmented surgically, cosmetically, and sartori-

*ally. Clothing is designed to accentuate these orifices and protuber-
ances, or at least to suggest their ready accessibility.*

*Names or logos of manufacturers are prominently displayed on
the more costly merchandise, advertising to the community (and
potential muggers) the wearer's disregard of price. Clothing design
also disregards comfort and avoids use of materials resistant to wear,
wrinkles, moisture, and stains.*

*Walking the streets is precarious because of foot and vehicle traf-
fic. Having excellent peripheral vision is vital to survival. This
highly evolved peripheral vision at first seemed in lieu of frontal
vision, but I had misunderstood. Their frontal vision is adequate,
but eye contact with other pedestrians is assiduously avoided perhaps
from fear of an attack or a request for help. Not even if you skip or
sing or offer an embrace will they respond. What strange,
unfriendly creatures! END OF NOTES*

Well, I'm impressed. I commend you for the effort at collect-
ing and interpreting information. That's actually quite good for
an alien. Of course, if you were a systems engineer, you would
recognize that the effectiveness, even survival, of any complex
system, including humans, is very dependent on the nature of
the system's inputs and outputs, since these are the vital links of
the system to its surroundings, its situation, and environment.
So yes, although I'd not thought of it in those terms, we pay
attention to our orifices. But that's not a fetish so much as the
reality that the orifices are gateways to our environment, the
links by which we arrive and survive, contribute, and procreate.
Do you understand what I'm saying to you?

*Yes, and I'm quite impressed that you are able to be both
instructive and paternalistic simultaneously. That must have taken
years of practice.*

Nonsense, I'm not the least bit paternalistic! You sound just like my daughter. Same time tomorrow?

OK.

SESSION 6

So let's recapitulate where we are in this mutual indoctrination. You see our planet about to self-destruct from run-amok technology, inept and venal leaders, and a culture with institutional structures hopelessly anachronistic owing to caveman legacies. You see me as parochial, paternalistic, provincial, and incapable of visualizing imminent catastrophe. I see you as arrogant, intrusive, critical, and without understanding, unduly pessimistic about my life and just a tad effeminate in your own. Does that about cover it?

Well, I'd say there's probably a touch of xenophobia, homophobia, and narcissism in your make-up also. But yes, I'd say that covers it rather well. Let me also mention that from my observations so far, I see you as a substantial cut above your fellow Earthlings in emotional and intellectual maturity.

Really?

Definitely. In fact, if there were more people like you around ... but frankly I don't see how you Earthlings have kept it together to this point. It's a real conundrum for me.

What do you mean?

Well, as soon as I recovered from what is roughly equivalent to jet-lag, I went looking for Earth's implosion triggers like I always do on this kind of mission. So of course that led me to America's post 9/11 behavior.

Excellent. That's where I'd start too, since the United States is the world's most powerful country and has adopted a purposeful, clearly enunciated—you said something about a conundrum?

Yes, I don't see how your intelligence people, given their dedication and resource ... well, I don't see how they could have permitted penetration by enemy agents to the highest levels of your government. These organizations must be riddled with widespread bribes, coercion and disinformation, still undetected.

Are you saying that enemy agents are running things here in America? That's preposterous.

How else can you explain the self-destructive policies of America's leadership and the absence of ongoing terrorist acts within the USA? Could mere venality or incompetence explain your leaders' choices of counterterrorism targets and strategies, their provocative rhetoric, divisive domestic policies, and haphazard effort toward domestic security? As inadequately prepared for their assignments as your leaders were, they are not stupid and have had time to learn from mistakes. So how else do you explain ...?

Do you really believe this sort of conspiracy nonsense?

I'm open to any alternative explanation. I even wondered if some of my people were playing a practical joke—we do that too, you know. I'm just saying that as a musicologist from out of town, things seem more than a little discordant here. How do you as a systems engineer begin to explain it?

Maybe you should get out more and look around again. OK, you identified a seeming paradox and then leaped to a Machiavellian super-spy explanation. Ludicrous! As a systems engineer, my first step would be to map the system's anatomy, identify its internal structure, its boundaries, external inputs, outputs, and stakeholders. Then I'd decide on the level of detail and which attributes to make explicit versus implicit. I would decide if my purpose was to redesign some system component or to resolve some conceptual paradox. If the latter, stakeholders' identity would need delineation such as their:

- roles and goals,

- resources and recourses,

- internal strengths and weaknesses,

- external threats and opportunities, and

- intentions and initiatives.

Interesting. In musicology, I also utilize an analytic process, a bit more implicit than explicit. Never mind. I'm comfortable with your approach; you'd already described it to me if you recall. So following it, I've laid everything out in a spreadsheet and now I'm more confused than before. The principle insight portrayed by my cluttered spreadsheet is the extreme diversity of the USA's recent initiatives: combating genocidal governments as in Bosnia, attacking Afghanistan ostensibly as 9/11 retribution, safeguarding oil sources as in Kuwait and Iraq.

What of Weapons of Mass Destruction (WMD), counterterrorism and pandemics? Isn't that why you're here?

Yes and they were in my first spreadsheet but then when I applied an overlay of behavior versus rhetoric it didn't work. It's a paradox. You've transformed my conundrum into a paradox!

Why, where's the paradox?

Well, since WMD, counterterrorism, and pandemics, not to mention drugs and money laundering, have all become global, that is, not containable within national borders, a sustained, mutual-trust international collaboration is obviously the essential starting point to accomplish anything. Yet the USA by word and deed has opposed global organizations and treaties in favor of a country-by-country approach. So your government doesn't appear to understand or be interested in its own survival somehow. Why not? Are you sure about your systems methodology? Look where it's taking me.

Yes, it's real, and now you're getting into the substantive implementation distinctions. "Insurgents" are especially troublesome when they form regional, common-cause coalitions. That's because the peacekeepers are nation-states historically organized to protect or steal gold, oil, or real estate from one-another. It's quite a nuisance to have to collaborate across national boundaries in detection and apprehension protocols, working out all their differences in surveillance technologies, rules of interrogation and engagement, civil rights, and law enforcement—not to mention sharing their private extortion files and their public blame and glory allocations. And because the established leaders are part of the establishment and have probably not been near poor people or direct combat, they don't understand how non-governmental enemies think or fight.

Also, quite often, what seems to create a paradox is traceable to mistaken identification of the true stakeholders and/or their characteristics.

I don't quite understand that.

For example, in various administrations at various times, there has been confusion as to whether the general public or special interests were the stakeholders primarily represented by the White House. Another example: it might be assumed that an airport is designed principally for the passengers or airlines, but often, it's really the airport's shop owners who are the dominant stakeholders in the airport's design. Another example is that frequently, a company is run for the benefit of its executive management rather than stockholders. I could go on.

Yes, you do.

Sometimes the anomaly lies with the system's level of aggregation. For example, mistreating prisoners may make tactical sense in combat, but not in fostering international goodwill, enemy desertions, or surrender. In our airport example, the principal stakeholders might harmonize their differences in designing and building the airport, only to find that local noise abatement officials, the stakeholders at a lower level of system aggregation, prohibit runway usage after 9 PM. Or in our company example, its executives and shareholders might be committed to quality products and satisfied customers, but the sales department accepts price and schedule contracts which leave no margin for product quality or customer satisfaction.

Got it. What appears paradoxical at one level of aggregation may make sense at another. Anything else?

Well, yes. Sometimes a seeming paradox is traceable to a conflict over resources or timing.

Timing?

Sure. For example, the field engineering team wants the product delivered in working order, complete with adequate training and documentation packages, tolerating late delivery if necessary. But the sales department wants to ship the product incomplete or untested, if necessary, but on time. The engineering production people might see a paradox in the directives they receive. Does all this make sense to you?

Yes, of course, but you surprise me. I'd have guessed that you tidy engineers would dislike paradoxes. And yet I hear you saying that the irritating paradox can be your invaluable friend, warning of misconceptions or of system flaws which you can then fix.

Right. And even if we can't fix them, we can at least deride them, demonstrating our erudition at staff meetings or cocktail parties.

Hmm, same time tomorrow?

Fine with me.

SESSION 7

I'm really getting a feel for your planet from the combination of walking around, your Internet, and our chats, of course. I'm even beginning to see the value of explicitly depicting complex situations as stakeholders and their systems. I also recognize your use of paradoxes to confirm concepts and/or to focus on "What's wrong with this picture?" as a very useful preamble to finding solutions. How about an example to illustrate some of this methodology?

Good idea. And I admit to learning some interesting things from you, too. I'm certainly intrigued with your imbedded sensory chip. Maybe we can develop one here.

I'd not encourage it. At Earth's level of civilization, it would probably become just one more abused addiction, a soporific just when you need all the intellectual energy you can muster. And given your primitive attempts at controlling addictions, whether drugs, religion, or whatever ... well, I'd wait a few more decades. Incidentally, my chip doesn't work here, probably because it's too far away from my home-base network.

That's too bad. OK, you wanted another example. Consider an office temperature control system. The heater is operated by the controller on the wall which keeps the heater on whenever room temperature drops below the desired set point. That's the system.

Good. It's so simple I don't even need the system diagram.

Yes. However, there are two principle stakeholders, the tenant and landlord, locked in protracted litigation. The landlord, appalled at the monthly heating bill, enters and lowers the temperature set point after the office vacates. The tenant resents the landlord's nightly entry and consequent chilly early mornings. His unsolicited advice to the landlord is to buy a modern, efficient heater. Meanwhile, office workers bring their individual heaters to work, which blow circuit breakers and cause computer, lighting and work stoppages. The landlord is suing to evict the tenant who is countersuing for trespassing and breach of lease contract.

Ridiculous! You Earthlings are so—does all that testosterone destroy your brain cells? It's a true paradox.

Well, yes and no. You might be thinking that the accrued legal costs are now several times the annual heating bill or cost of installing double-pane, insulated windows or a time-programmable temperature regulator. But the landlord is prohibited from changing windows without bringing everything up to building code, and film insulation for one window will have other tenants demanding the same enhancement. Changing the regulator will trigger a visit from the insurance and fire inspectors, which is always an unpredictable, often traumatic, event.

All right then, what about the tenant? Isn't he behaving immaturely?

Not if he runs a security software firm which must carefully screen visitors to the premises. I'm not saying it's not the testosterone. I'm merely pointing out that detailing, maybe even diagramming, the system and it's stakeholders at selectable levels might help the hapless arbitrator if the litigators are wise enough to use one. It could organize the discourse, suggest design or conceptual possibilities and/or demystify seeming paradoxes, even for this simple system problem. Such simple tools as spreadsheets are invaluable for comparing stakeholder advantages for each alternative. Here, I've constructed one for our example. I'll send it to you as an e-mail attachment.

STAKEHOLDERS → ALTERNATIVES ↓	OWNER	TENANT	EMPLOYEES	CONTRACTOR	INSURER
LITIGATE LEASE					
INSULATE WINDOWS					
UPGRADE HEATER					
UPGRADE REGULATOR					

Got it. Incidentally, in your terminology, can a stakeholder be an organization as well as an individual or group?

Yes, and sometimes the paradox can be traced to conflicting goals internal to the stakeholder. An individual may be seeking both gratification and pain avoidance by other-than-complementary routes. Or within a single stakeholder organization, the Federal Aviation Administration, for example, is simultaneously charged with both regulating and promoting the airline industry.

What? You're pulling my antenna. How can that work? Do any of your other organizations have this same kind of inconsistency?

Certainly. The Department of Agriculture must promote yet regulate agriculture. The Department of Transportation, the

Federal Communications Commission, and several of the Homeland Security Offices all have these mission anomalies. But along with the chaos and confusion come synergies and serendipities of value. The retired military officer who becomes a defense firm's research director brings an intimate understanding of unmet military needs and potential sponsors of future research breakthroughs.

Are you serious? It sounds totally disorganized, something that would invite waste, fraud, and abuse galore.

Well, yes, I suppose you can look at it that way. But every system has its anomalies, both complementary and conflicting. In a marriage system, with the bride as a principal stakeholder, her purpose might be children and a house, whereas the groom-stakeholder's purpose might be increased copulation competence and frequency. With goodwill and communication they should be able to harmonize their respective purposes.

Are there any other anomalies regarding stakeholders and paradoxes?

There's the past-present-future trichotomy. All private firms and most government agencies have to make trade-off choices between being prepared to accomplish future missions while at the same time performing well in the present. This requires working today in a way that doesn't create undue turmoil with the past, or jeopardize the future.

Have you an example to clarify this?

Sure, several. The Defense Department expends substantial resources to maintain very large, costly programs of no direct relevance to its future missions. This preserves continuity of programs and capabilities, employment and relationships, both for internal agency and external political exigencies. In turn, a vigorous, competent, cooperative defense industry is preserved and program management skills are retained within the department.

Conversely, to exploit a revolutionary idea might require success of an unproven technology, an extended development time, and/or an uncertain cost for meeting a challenge that may never materialize. Whether that risky idea with its futuristic payoff should be allowed to deplete funds and management attention from more immediate needs creates another kind of time-related conflict.

The trade-offs must be excruciating, and it sounds grossly inefficient. I assume your private firms are more efficient and focused on their future needs and opportunities.

Well, large private firms, allegedly more nimble and efficient in personnel and resource utilization, behave similarly when grappling with the same kind of past-present-future stress. Larger firms often nurture a residue of revered but obsolete products, technologies, sales strategies, and executives. The executives also tend to have a conservative bias, a reluctance to deviate from what worked before, what works now and their current status, all for an unproven future initiative.

What about small, new firms?

Small firms, particularly those with high-tech products or a specialized market niche that permits high-profit pricing ... such firms can and do tolerate incredibly disorganized, poorly managed operations. Sometimes a cavalier attitude develops, ignoring lessons learned and current customers in favor of "staying ahead" with new products, technologies, and markets. Disappointments are dealt with by "political gestures," such as firing the sales manager. Orderly organization and processes aren't opposed; they're just not seen as important. In some instances, even focusing on organization and finance is per-

ceived as an insulting lack of appreciation for the firm's proprietary technologies and products.

*This is all quite weird. I think I'd better walk around some more
to clear my proboscis and get a first-hand look at what you have
been chattering about. And as you have taught me, I intend to pay
attention to stakeholders' goals and roles, resources and recourses,
anomalies and homilies, intentions and pretensions. I'm thinking of
composing a libretto ... ☺*

If you're serious, take a look at our airline industry. But don't
get cute or even reveal that you're a musicologist, or else the key
people will ignore you. This industry exemplifies what solid systems engineering can accomplish, i.e., a safe, fast, efficient transportation system supplied by a healthy, technology-driven
industry, harmonizing a diverse set of stakeholders. Such
accomplishments don't just happen. Intelligent, vigilant, adaptable systems engineering, a balanced relationship between government regulators, equipment suppliers, airlines, and more are
required ...

You're being uncharacteristically quiet. So what are you
thinking?

*Your mapping salient attributes of key stakeholders, their mis-
sions, capabilities, intentions, and their connections to the system
are obviously valuable and not too difficult. But then knowing who
they are, where they could go, and where they think they're going.
That all seemed excessively tedious and superfluous at first. Now,
given all the seeming contradictions, and the networks' synergistic
and competing linkages, I get that it is complicated and not just at
the policy level. Your mapping process must be useful and probably
works down through small organizations and even relationships*

Excellent! I'm proud of you. Anything else?

Just this: you're not quite as nerdy as I'd thought. Tomorrow, regular time?

Right.

SESSION 8

Now about your airline industry, I have some notes I'll email to you.

Fine, and thanks for that last comment before you signed off—almost friendly. Keep it up and you're liable to be invited over for a beer and Monday Night Football.

Why, thank you. That's quite gracious of you. And while on the topic I've wondered if the widespread popularity of watching Monday Night Football derives primarily from having avoided being a combatant on the field? I'm sure that spectators of violence in ancient coliseums, modern opera houses, and bullfights share the same motivation. So it can't be the beer. If you can explain that, then please tell me about the mass appeal of watching your non-combat sports, like baseball.

I understand what you're saying. My ex-wife thought that watching baseball was almost as exciting as watching paint dry. But as for football, speaking man to man, it's sort of like sex. You can never quite explain it; you just have to experience it. Tell you what. Come on over next Monday night. It's the Oakland Raiders versus the Patriots—you'll see a massacre. I'll have a few of the guys in. With some beer and pretzels, I think you'll begin to get the feel of it.

Thanks, but maybe another time. So moving right along, you suggested looking at your airline industry. I did and here are my notes of some of my first impressions. I invite your critique since I'm such a neophyte here.

Your modesty becomes you and is almost credible. Where's your e-mail attachment? Ah, here it comes.

NOTES: This planet's air transportation incorporates large numbers of passenger and cargo aircraft. Their global system manages air traffic, collision avoidance, navigation, maintenance, security and various airport functions. It's all integrated, reliable, and relatively inexpensive. Clearly sophisticated technologies of aerodynamics, systems management, propulsion, telecommunications, and flight control have been used.

So I'm impressed, but also puzzled. They use human flight crews. But autopilots and automatic takeoff and landing systems are entirely adequate, often better than human performance. Emergency systems would be far better if automated, functionally and in terms of comparative cost, weight and space. But they continue to use a human flight crew. Here's an instance where available, advantageous technology goes unused. Why?

And another thing: their takeoff and landing runways are just long, linear strips of concrete! I recall observing them from home and puzzling over what they might be. Now that I know, I'm puzzling over why it's done this way instead of using contoured circular or spiraled runways to conserve land, recycle takeoff-landing energy and retain the shock absorption and aerodynamic braking mechanisms in the runway rather than on board! I'm surprised there's any space and weight allowance available for passengers. And the glide path must be unforgiving and excruciatingly precise—that's insane!

The airport's land cost, noise, and smell force its location away from population centers. Accordingly, accessing the airport requires as much time and adrenalin as the flight itself. The discomfited passenger barely gets to the airport in time to relieve stress by visiting the shops and bars. Why are passengers so docile or powerless?

Even as a musicologist, I can see some other technology anachronisms worth noting. On this planet the designers use enormously protruding, rigid wing structures—possibly inspired by their preoccupation with sexual symbolism. Haven't they noticed how birds fly?

Propulsion? Engine designers evidently believe that the earth will never run out of fossil fuel, since they use it everywhere. Well, they could be right; the supply may outlast them. Then there's all the noise, vibration, and heat from those engines. I guess it scares the pigeons away.

Earthlings have valuable but idle technologies on the one hand, and manifestly solvable technology bottlenecks on the other. Why is that? It may be that their regulatory agencies are so concerned with safety, noise abatement, and self-protection that exploiting advanced technologies with long-term payoff doesn't get much attention. It may be that the aircraft suppliers are locked into the tradition of relying on military programs for advances in aerodynamics, structure, and propulsion technologies.

Oh, I almost forgot. There's also something called a "helicopter," probably inspired by a high-school science project. I can't describe it without sounding deranged. A pilot told me that designers are trying to make them fly at speeds and altitudes like a real airplane but I think he was just testing my gullibility. END OF NOTES.

Your points are well-taken, but I can explain it all. Fundamentally, the rigid wings we use must fly at high speed for the airflow to provide the necessary lift and control. Attaining the necessary takeoff speed and decelerating from the equally demanding touch-down speed necessitate the mile-long runways. Then the resulting aerodynamic forces impose structural requirements on the aircraft, adding more weight, which calls for more lift, hence a larger, heavier wing, and so forth. Adding in shock and vibration considerations, you can imagine the consequent demands on everything else, such as landing gear, engines, and hydraulics. A flight engineer friend confided that every time his aircraft touches down he hears an inner-voice exclaiming, "Wow, another miracle."

That said, I'd like to add that our specific knowledge of materials and design may be primitive compared to yours. But what may seem ludicrous to you may seem quite ingenious to us—just as some of your observations may seem clever and insightful to you, but rude and gratuitous to us.

You are quite right, and I apologize for the snide tone of my personal notes. It's how I converse with myself. I'll continue, both of us mindful that these are informal, rough notes only and that I'm continuing to express myself in your style as best I can.

Fair enough. If you'll let me, I can help with some of your misconceptions. For example, yes our "aircraft have to carry complex, heavy landing gear and brake/boost capabilities and all that aerodynamic readjustment paraphernalia," simply because runways don't facilitate those functions. But please understand that early aircraft were small, slow and unreliable. Being able to land on a road or a vacant field was important. Subsequent aircraft, airports, and the industry evolved accordingly.

Now with hundreds of different types of aircraft and airports, a complete change-over would be financially impossible, available technologies notwithstanding.

OK, that's helpful. Does history also explains the anachronism of retaining human flight crews, although your computers are far more compact, reliable, inexpensive, and versatile? It must be something else.

No. I think it's just that passengers feel more comfortable entrusting their lives to some humans in the cockpit than to computers.

No offense, but when it comes to flying, you Earthlings are weird and superstitious as well!

How so?

For example, before boarding, you walk under magnetic arches, religious counselors tell you to remove jackets or shoes and some worshippers raise their arms emulating angels. You carry bulky bags even though most of the contents could be acquired at the destination. Some bags are quite heavy, but if checked rather than hand-carried aboard they may not be x-rayed, which I presume confers some sort of sanctification of personal property. On board, some pray into small, wireless communication devices and then fasten seat belts as if that would protect them should the aircraft fall 30,000 feet into the sea. Strange creatures.

No, no, no. You've got it all wrong. Let me explain.

Don't bother. To paraphrase my favorite systems engineer, let's move to a higher level of aggregation—or would that be aggravation?

Look, this is serious. Please don't try to be funny about it.

OK, but for your information, on my planet we take humor very seriously. We use it in many non-trivial ways. It can indicate emotional maturity, objectivity, even stability. You seldom see an anarchist smile or crack a joke.

Please …

OK. Back to work. Here's my more general conundrum: air travel serves an elite, upscale market, more able to absorb costs of modernization than ground transportation. So the advantages of advanced technology should be more visible and economically viable. What takes it so long to be applied?

From an engineering perspective, I grant you that some of our technologies are indeed marginal, imposing stringent safety requirements and therefore rigid safety standards in design and operations. The standards are regulated by bureaucracies that inherently constrain introduction of new technologies. No matter how lucrative the projections appear, changes in "turf" boundaries are resisted. So are programs with long-term payback of initial investments and which have no immediate payback for the incumbent stakeholders.

But isn't your aircraft industry motivated and powerful enough to overcome these barriers?

That used to puzzle me, too. What happened is that just a very few firms have come to dominate the industry, initially by innovative technology and programming. But once they "own" the dominant market share, ironically, they discourage new technology. Backed by the aerospace and insurance industries, manufacturers prefer to sell the same standard products with minimal changes.

You're telling me that both the dominant private sector firms and government regulators are inherently change-averse?

I think you've got that right. You can see it reflected in the inept way we deal with terrorism threats to aircraft. If budgets were allocated strictly according to the cost-effectiveness of available countermeasures verses threat probabilities, all devoid of political or public relations considerations, the programmatic initiatives would look quite different from how it's handled today.

Fascinating! I'm thinking that your referring me to your aircraft industry was not as casual a suggestion as it sounded. That industry seems to exemplify the barriers to changing a global system containing a multiplicity of entrenched markets, products, and protocols. Those barriers would seem to be sociopolitical and institutional more than economic and technological. Will I find this same pattern in other industries?

When their bureaucracies and infrastructures are set in concrete, and their insurance carriers are more influential than their S&T community, absolutely. Look at urban housing and mass transit, or nuclear power plants, as other examples. So you and I are not likely to overemphasize the challenges to effectuating changes needed for a stable future here.

That must be very frustrating for a logical systems engineer such as you. Consulting in these sectors must call for patience and euphemisms galore.

Yes. I've learned to smile and say "Isn't your position somewhat short-sighted?" when I want to say something like "Have you considered rest and medication?" That reminds me, it's getting late and I'm due for some rest and medication at my favorite neighborhood bar. Tomorrow, same time?

With pleasure. Have fun tonight.

SESSION 9

My Internet server conked out for an hour this morning. So while I was waiting, I browsed through our past e-mail messaging and again noticed how alike we sound. It's a bit weird. Do all you ETs express yourselves like an Earthling engineer?

No, not at all. At home, our style is more abbreviated, direct and without much nuance or ambiguity, but with lots of humor, especially puns. We value integrity and humor, so our communication must reflect that. I believe I'd mentioned that we automatically adopt the vocabulary and speech structures of anyone in close communication. Even when I've just been walking around here, I keep my notes in the same tone as our conversations. I hope it's not too confusing to you. So tell me more about systems.

Fine, but first, I wanted to mention that your impressions of the airline industry are excellent; more sophisticated than some of your earlier walking-around comments. At some point you might want to look at our ground transportation too. Its served market isn't as elite as our air transport, so its broader profile may better convey what our planet is and isn't.

I look forward to it. Hopefully my comments will be well-grounded if not air-udite. ☺

OK, enough pun fun for today. Before we start, another question keeps gnawing at me. How and why did you get to me? Was it just random luck?

It can't be, and I'm as puzzled as you are. For this sort of activity we use what for you would be a highly sophisticated computerized search and evaluation program. I'd have expected to be directed to a biophysicist or any of a variety of real specialists. Instead I get—tell me what's special about you?

Sure, but first let me mention something special about you. Almost every question you direct to me includes an insult or a put-down. Is this a personal antagonism, or are you just generally obnoxious? Did your colleagues really send you here on this mission or was it just that you're such a pain in the ass to be around? It's a good thing we're in a chat room rather than the same room or I'd probably have punched you out at the start of this nonsense.

How charming! Thanks for the reminder.

What reminder?

That you're still barbarians here! You have just enough technology to have provided the façade of culture and civilization. What arrogance! Look at how you'd resolve our differences: punching me out. And to think I was starting to—never mind, let's get on with it. You're making me feel lonely and homesick, which is weird because those are Earthling feelings that we never—let's get on with it.

Right. Since we're being candid, I'd have expected they'd send a team of well-trained, tough experts on this sort of assignment, not a musicologist sounding like my ex-wife with PMS. It seems like you ET guys could use a bit more testosterone yourselves. OK, like you say, let's get on with it. You were asking what's special about me. What's special about me is that I'm a multidimensional hybrid with a combined background of management and engineering consulting in academia and business, government and non-government entities.

Fine. I hope you've acquired some wisdom in the process that can help us along here. Even as a multidimensional hybrid you must have learned some invaluable lessons.

Look; we don't need to keep doing this. In fact, one of my important, almost proprietary "lessons learned" is that wisdom may get verbalized and even transmitted. But it doesn't get accepted, digested, integrated, reinforced, and utilized devoid of context and empathy exchanged with the sender. My ex-wife and I conducted interminable, intellectual discussions from our respective knowledge bases, but little wisdom was exchanged because the reinforcing empathy wasn't—sorry, I got off on a bit of digression, but I'm sure you get my point.

Touché. I apologize for my outburst. This planet, or our dialog, seem to stir feelings in me that we regard as primitive and ludicrous back home; it takes getting used to, I guess. Never mind. Let's continue. Tell me some insights learned from your work.

OK, here's one. Managers do well at what I call "curator" management. Their academic training focuses them on managing the interior of the organization with the underlying assumption that the past is prologue to the future, and that if anything important changes it will do so slowly enough and "linearly." This works fine for office camaraderie. But the vital management challenges, both threats and opportunities, usually emanate from outside the organization and are seldom predictable from merely projecting the past. Conversely, some challenges just pop up from details below the manager's radar screen.

Whether from outside or from the overlooked interior, the "surprise" could have been dealt with better had contingency planning and resources been in place. But the typical manager wasn't looking ahead, or outside, or deeply within the organization. Even when contingency planning is in place, it is usually focused on the dramatic but unlikely catastrophe, ignoring the more prosaic yet probable eventualities.

Interesting. Another example?

Sure. Entrepreneurial management, whether a new start-up, shut-down, or major operational change is difficult because successful implementation usually requires all the elements to be in place or coordinated at the outset. Opening a new restaurant requires that the facility, the staff and its training, fixtures, food purchasing, marketing, finance, and regulatory certifications; everything must be functioning at the start.

Then, as challenging as this implementation is, getting the conceptual part right is vital as well. The entrepreneur must understand how things work and how to make things work. What unique attributes can I bring to my restaurant or its marketing that will produce the intended result? How might competitors retaliate?

And you contend that applying your systems methodologies obviates these difficulties? Please tell me more about your systems methodologies. I'm sure you do more than just a meticulous job of mapping the stakeholders and their characteristics. There must be more.

Of course, once again, depending on our purpose and intention, we usually need to explicitly detail the system including the system's relevant inputs and outputs, both desired and not.

Desired and not?

Yes. For example, if we have designated the jet engine as our system, this system's desired output is thrust. Its noise and heat outputs, as well as its substantial vibration, are some of its undesired outputs. Its fuel and maintenance are some of the intended inputs. Some of these inputs and outputs might be irrelevant to our analysis or design purpose and consequently not included for consideration.

As another example, consider a business as the designated system. Its outputs include customer products, shareholder dividends, and more, all deriving from its inputs of materials, sales orders, technologies, labor, and capital. Depending on our purpose and available information, which determine how accurately we must portray the company as a system, we choose the relevant inputs/outputs for inclusion.

That sounds a bit arbitrary. What's next?

For any such example we can construct a model of the system's anatomy, including explicit or implicit representation of the system's interior, its subsystems and components and their interconnections. Our model might be mathematical or an actual prototype, from which we can then test or optimize the design, predict performance results, use the model as a training tool or blueprint for construction. All sorts of neat things.

So why, then, do the systems I've observed seem so unsystematic and precarious?

Well, if from knowing or controlling the stakeholders, you have the luxury of designing the system structure and its subsystems, you can make it as systematic and rugged as budget and schedule permit. If you either don't know or can't control some of these system elements, you can design in redundancies or self-adaptive procedures. You have lots of choices, but you must know what you don't know and what to do about it in order to get the design that works. Similarly the people who operate within the system or maintain and fix it when it becomes operational, or revise it as needed, they've got to know what they know and adjust appropriately for any lack of knowledge or competencies.

They've got to have the right conceptual models. People within the system must understand its purpose and the outputs or consequences of the applied inputs sufficiently to perform their functions. Most important, they must recognize when the system's exterior or interior have changed and how to respond. Otherwise you have a very unsystematic, precarious situation. If anticipated, you can design around some of this ignorance and/ or malevolence, otherwise watch out!

That's so general, you've lost me. Can you give me an example or two?

Sure, but I'm already late for a meeting. Let's pick it up tomorrow. Regular time, OK?

That's fine. Tomorrow.

SESSION 10

You asked for an example or two. So I went back over our last chat and I can appreciate your request. I do get wound up in endless generalities. Sorry, and in the future, please tell me when I do that.

That's very considerate of you. Your meeting yesterday must have been successful, putting you in a thoughtful mood.

Not quite. My "meeting" was actually a blind date arranged by a friend.

Why? What happened? I know it's none of my business, but I need to learn about how you Earthlings behave with each other at the individual as well as institutional level.

Sure, no big deal. Putting it very simply, on a date I either want to get educated, entertained, or laid. It may be that you and me, our chatting, has been raising the hurdle too high for the first two to be satisfied elsewhere or maybe somehow I'm starting to want all three in one relationship. I don't know.

I find this fascinating and appreciate your candor.

Yeah, well either as a joke to reduce tension or as a device to check me out, my blind date was wearing one of those t-shirts captioned "WITH THESE, WHO NEEDS A BRAIN?" After chuckling and ordering drinks, somehow I kept drifting off—actually, trying to think of some good system examples for you and me to discuss.

So if your evening produced some good examples, it wasn't entirely a waste of time.

Well, here's one example that came to mind. It illustrates the importance of having the right conceptual model and/or recognizing when you don't and then what to do about it. There was a farmer whose frugality inspired the objective of training his plow horse to stop eating. His strategy was to decrease the horse's daily feed by an imperceptible 1 percent. But just as the farmer had almost reached his goal, the horse died. OK, that's just a joke, but we're all like that farmer.

That's ridiculous. Even Earthlings aren't that naïve. Wouldn't the farmer have recognized as the horse became weak and ill that his underlying concept was wrong and needed to be replaced?

Not necessarily. We often find it difficult to perceive and digest information that threatens our concept or committed position. As a systems engineer, I can tell you of countless examples in which hard facts and fresh data lose out to nostalgia or ego rigidities.

Yes, I've observed that about you Earthlings. If in doubt about the future, you seem comfortable with a so-far-so-good posture. I've wondered if this tendency toward linear extrapolation derives from the need to assume immortality in order to make it through the day.

Hmm, now that's a weird but interesting notion. To continue, acknowledging a changed situation may compel a response with disconcerting risks and uncertainties. So denying or ignoring the change, that is, overlooking the proverbial elephant-in-the-room; that's a more pervasive reaction than might be expected. We may not starve a horse, but we often starve or overfeed a relationship, an investment, or a military campaign. We steadfastly reject forewarnings of change until there is a sharp metamorphosis or context upset which can no longer be ignored.

The horse died; enlightenment came too late. But what if signs portending the future had been observed, accepted, and acted upon with a timely, effective remedy? Here's an example of what I mean. It happens to be real.

A large company's strategy for dominating its labor unions consisted of denigrating and dividing union management while threatening workers with layoffs, very effectively intimidating and controlling its workforce. But gradually a series of increasingly potent work stoppages, plus associated bad press and governmental regulatory attention, began to seriously threaten the company. Efforts to publicly humiliate the union leadership backfired, generating empathy and solidarity among the rank-and-file union members.

Had our oblivious farmer been in charge, the company would have eventually died. But thoughtful executives of the company and of the unions recognized that the situation had changed. Each side was now fundamentally vulnerable to the other. Their respective top executives not only understood this, but accordingly committed to a major change: replacing the unilateral intimidation strategy with a functional bargaining process.

Recognizing that the situation had changed was difficult and only accepted after a protracted strike had substantially damaged both the company and its unions. Deciding on a course of action and gaining its consensus was greatly facilitated by perceiving and portraying the situation as a system, replete with its stakeholders, interacting subsystems, and components, all of it.

Implementing the new bargaining process took time and consistent authority to enforce the agreed-upon "rules of engagement." Vigilance, understanding, and patience with a series of mutual confidence-building steps were essential. Many of those affected wouldn't or couldn't see the big picture, that is, the system of many interacting components at several different levels. Many could not see or believe in the need for change and/or how to adapt to this radically different process.

That must be why I see many obviously counterproductive yet persistent conflicts here. Effectuating change, particularly in your large, complex systems, involves not only known risks but unknowable risks. I'd guess that potential rewards and their perceived benefits are similarly uncertain, hence discounted in the anticipation.

Quite right. Resistance to change is inevitable, so the implementers must be able to assure that the change's risk/reward will be favorable. Perceived risk/reward will differ with location, organizational level, and local cultures. Insensitivity to such differences will result in lots of dead horses.

Same time tomorrow?

Certainly

SESSION 11

I haven't heard from you for a few days. Has your social life become more diverting?

Not exactly. I felt a need to take a break. If you must know, I got into a bit of a tiff with my friend, the guy who introduced me to the t-shirt woman. He wanted to know how the date went and somehow I started talking about having been distracted thinking about my ET, and he started to laugh, then got angry and told me to get my life orthogonal again. Did I mention he's an engineer too? He suggested that you and I meet, implying that might get the cobwebs out of my hard drive, and then he stalked off. So I felt I needed the weekend to hike, meditate and argue things out with Teresa and Sam—sorry, I should have e-mailed you.

Well, I was starting to worry. Teresa and Sam, your children?

No, just tropical goldfish; the residue of my community property. Would you like to meet them?

Not especially, but what about our meeting? Your friend may have made a good suggestion.

60

Sure, let's meet for dinner. I assume you're near or can get to my neighborhood easily?

Not a problem.

Great. My favorite place is "Sports and Steaks." We can meet there. It has a men's club atmosphere and a great selection of premium beer. But first, I've got to ask—you indicated that you're able to walk around undetected as an extraterrestrial. I assume you're kidding about your proboscis and antenna, right?

Yes, of course. In fact, physiologically, we are almost identical to Earth people even without a protoplasm adaptation touch-up. I have one but haven't had to use it since arrival.

Are you certain we are so similar? How do you know? Have you been hanging out at one of our locker-rooms?

No. That might be awkward for me. But I have seen some of your so-called "adult films." So I know that structurally, if not romantically, we're identical. This may be the time to reveal that choosing your planet, among others on the verge of extinction, was influenced by this virtual identity of our respective species and the planet characteristics that caused identical evolutionary outcomes— juxtaposed in time, of course, which explains our more-advanced culture, and emotional and intellectual maturity.

But certainly not tact. So what did you think of the films?

At first, I felt sorry for the actors—how demeaning for them, forced to pretend enjoyment and affection. Then I felt sorry for the viewers—how boring for them. Then I remembered that you Earthlings, lacking a sensory-fusion cerebral implant must derive stimulation and gratification from externalities via your senses: seeing, hearing, smelling, and touching. How cumbersome! It begins to explain how extraordinarily appetite-driven your cultures are, even after the basics of food, shelter, and health care are provided.

Interesting observation but I'm not sure you have the complete picture. In any case, let's get back to management and systems engineering. I'm glad you look like an ordinary guy from Earth, but guys aren't very interesting. Systems are.

All right, have you another example besides the farmer-horse failure and the company-union success?

Well, Iraq is an interesting example. It's virtually the opposite of the company example we were discussing.

Oh?

Yes. In the Iraq situation, we had all the resources and recourses available, thanks to 9/11 reactions, plus decades of accrued trust and goodwill internationally, a strong economy and military. The situation was unique in having so many positive factors at the external, executive, and policy levels. Moreover, the key stakeholders were in alignment as to the initiatives to undertake despite disparities among the original objectives, i.e., to find WMD, to bring about regime change, to install democracy and military bases, to secure oil sourcing, and to project regional power.

That sounds good.

Yes, except that the key managers didn't have a realistic perception of the crucial inputs, nor understanding of what the inputs would produce as system outputs—"transfer functions" to engineers.

You're saying their expectations were unrealistic?

Yes. Unrealistic in the extreme:

- that a powerful initial attack would destroy or otherwise inhibit subsequent military responses;

- that Iraq's oil revenues would fund the undertaking;

- that adjacent countries would be intimidated or otherwise cooperative;

- that democracy would spring forth spontaneously, suppressing traditional ethnic and tribal conflicts;

- that existing satellite and human intelligence on the ground would suffice;

- that friends and allies of the past would rally 'round;

- that linkages of Iraq to WMD and bin Laden would be discovered;

- that control of information and staying the course would work long enough to prevail before doubts and eroding loyalties would ensue.

They got all of them wrong.

Were there no experts warning of the impending situation if implemented as planned?

Yes, even some common-sense non-experts.

Once underway, didn't the leaders quickly identify and correct their system input-output misconceptions?

We don't do that very quickly here, especially in large, highly visible political systems. In political or military conflict, changing course carries the risk of appearing weak or indecisive or inept, hence the reluctance to do so. Moreover, the key decision-makers' conceptual approach, rationale, and strategies all were based on some solid successes in history. The memory of past successes probably reinforced a "stay the course" posture despite the excruciating reality that the world had now changed. It's complicated.

This is unreal. Did they meet any of their goals in this period?

Absolutely. Political solidarity and consumer and investor confidence were maintained steadfast in America and Britain. The public's concerns about governmental ineptitude and threats to the economy, including trade deficits and unemployment, investor confidence, and even the budget deficit were successfully deflected or postponed. Warnings of dangerous international reactions, nuclear proliferation, increased global warming, and genocide were muted, encapsulated or ignored.

Anything else?

Well, yes. Institutions and programs historically associated with previous administrations were successfully weakened: progressive taxation, reforms of election financing and fraud, support of the UN and World Bank, diplomacy with some unfriendly countries, science policy, and support of some key treaties. I can understand how you might infer a malevolent conspiracy from all this. But I am convinced that leaders in the United States and Great Britain believed that what they were doing was best for their countries, and by extension, the world.

Amazing! So, in light of your answers to my last questions, don't you see the plausibility of my pessimism about planet Earth's future? Even if the highest, most powerful leaders are not malevolent, merely misguided, incompetent, and unable to learn and change, what chance does your planet have in confronting the even more serious challenges ahead?

Well, not many of my fellow Earthlings have your experience with planet disintegration. I would suggest, however, that we possess the insights, knowledge, and capabilities to figure it all out and fix it. We just need to be alerted to the threat, given the information and resources to work the problem, and help implement the solution. We would start with a retrospective system analysis....

Oh? Please spare me the details. What might the results of that look like?

Well, I'd have to actually do it to know for sure, but it might come out something like this. The ostensible system purpose for the Iraq-Afghanistan war was counterterrorism, i.e. destroying or deactivating terrorists, gratifying constituents' cry for 9/11 retaliation, and power projection.

However, the White House inner circle's almost total lack of experience in foreign policy, and in indigenous cultures and institutions of the Middle East; this lack of experience was a substantial handicap. Prior credentials in the Washington-military nexus, in aerospace systems and global strategy; such experience while reassuring, proved largely irrelevant to managing counterterrorism, ground warfare, and tactical intelligence. They didn't even target the countries where the 9/11 terrorist organizations originated or found refuge. As a result:

- The "inner-circle" team overestimated global receptivity to their lofty purposes and underestimated the motivated, effective opposition.

- Steadfast commitment to preconceived ideas, together with unwavering conviction of military omnipotence, blinded them to vulnerabilities and to realistic strategies as events unfolded.

- For homeland security the team leaders took the politically appealing approach of patching together existing activities under a single organization rather than designing a new organization to meet the new challenges.

- For whatever reasons, egotism, emotional or intellectual conviction, concern over the PR affects of changing course, ignorance, loyalties, whatever—they stayed on course as long as possible, avoiding corrective action until too late.

- Meanwhile, the actual military campaigns exacerbated the terrorism threat, alienated internal and external entities that might have helped, and failed to locate any WMD. Almost all wars reflect some miscalculations, rejection of bad news, and mindless rigidities. Exacerbating this one was the unprecedented speed and coverage of the mass media, which eroded confidence at home and helped strengthen and guide opposition elsewhere. Together with the leadership's reluctance to partner with other countries or build competence by bringing in outside experts; that reluctance proved disastrous.

That sounds terrible. Is that why you chose this example for me?
Yes, terrible it is. I chose it because it embodies virtually all the system flaws we might normally encounter. That's convenient for our discussion, even though it makes systems methodologies appear more cumbersome than in the more usual situation where you have just one or two flaws to confront.

Usually when a paradox invites you to do a complex top-down system design review, you find the flaw. The stakeholder's purposes may conflict, or some stakeholders may have been overlooked, or the most powerful stakeholders may not be communicating with the necessary experts and information analysts. Often, there are flaws within the system structure, missing or inadequate subsystems or misallocation of mandates, that sort of thing. Often there are misconceptions about what inputs are necessary to produce the designated subsystem outputs and the system lacks responsive mechanisms for correcting such flaws. What's your reaction to all this?

My impression is that it's a multi-faceted situation and especially unique in that the bus driver stays on the road that passengers recognize doesn't go to the driver's stated destination. Is it reality denial, fear-induced paralysis, inability to process such a new situation? I can't tell. In any case I'd say that when the destination or the road to it is wrong and lessons from past errors are not utilized, the driver or passengers should get off that bus. Otherwise ...

Otherwise?

Otherwise, update your resume and passport, sell your stocks, and buy gold. ☺

Clever, but not very amusing to me. So how about dinner Monday night at 8:00? I've reserved my regular table. Details as attached.

That's fine. I look forward to our meeting. Now, I have more questions about your Iraq example.

No. Right now I don't want to talk about this further. You are enjoying the inquiry almost as a scholar. For me, it is extremely painful. I feel as if my country has been betrayed and stolen by enemies, as you initially speculated. The reality is embarrassing to any aware person who cherishes civilization, but it is also very painful, like the death of a loved one. So please, let's move on. Same time tomorrow?

Certainly, and forgive my insensitivity. Your chat rooms are great for messaging. But body language and facial expressions don't translate very well and sometimes they're important. Again, my apologies.

SESSION 12

I've continued to follow your advice of looking around, and each time I come back with more questions. In particular, your housing and transportation, conveyance of money, energy, and information all seem archaic to the point of ... well, it draws me back to conspiracy theories again and even some sympathy for your leaders who may be trying to manage the unmanageable.

Now it's my turn to ask: what in the world you are talking about?

Let's start with housing. Help me to understand home ownership as your people deal with it.

That's an easy one. Whether there's an instinctual component evolved from caveman days or not, we all feel the need for a home. It's expressed somewhat differently at childhood, at parenting, and at old age. Even when searching for a mate, it appears muted, but isn't really. The teenager yearning for privacy and independence or the student away at college leaves a "Don't touch my room!" message. Don't you find that on other planets?

Yes, of course. The need for a home is universal. What's odd is that here people seem to need to own the structure that houses it; even the ground around and under it, none of which is even part of home per se. I find that very odd, like needing to own the cow in order to enjoy milk.

What's odd about it? The alternative of renting involves monthly payments that don't add value and there's always a landlord to appease.

But the numbers I've seen suggest that the structure and land are very costly for a family, even with your tax subsidies from mortgage interest. Except in high-growth areas, the resale profit from market appreciation seems generally negligible after adjusting for inflation and taxes, operating costs, and equity opportunity costs. All these combine to make house ownership exorbitant.

Well OK, if that's what the average numbers say. Incidentally, are you an economist or a musicologist?

I'm definitely a musicologist, but at home, we're all exposed to enough arithmetic for rudimentary consumer and political self-protection. And primitive as it is, your Internet makes information acquisition easy if you know what to look for.

Interesting. Have you any other observations about our "house ownership" aberrations?

Yes! Even more important than the financials, you sacrifice mobility, which impacts employment opportunities, commute time, and leverage with local government, which in turn affects the quality of schools, crime fighting, and public transportation. On our planet ownership consists only of some furniture and fixtures, the floor and wall coverings. If residents are unhappy with the community, they can pack their personal possessions and leave.

Our combination of high-rise multiple-housing structures and mobility for proximity to schools, recreation, and jobs avoids your "soccer mom and school bus" schedules and other time-wasting obligations. Why do Earthlings so readily accept these ludicrous commuting expenditures of time, money, and schedule rigidities?

Finally, I don't understand your land and air usage. In our cities, homes are stacked 50–100 units high, which conserves ground for parks and recreation and minimizes costs of security, utilities, construction, maintenance, and traffic flow.

Hmm, I suppose it's because our consumer lacks the mathematical sophistication to reach your conclusions, which certainly run contrary to what the construction, mortgage, insurance, and real estate industries all advise. Then, too, homeowners find value in conforming to the community culture of home ownership. I guess that when we want to own a house badly enough, we unconsciously adjust our estimated future earning power, appreciation, and inflation rates to make the numbers come out as we want them to. Incidentally, we do go vertical in planned or high population-density areas from time to time. Anything else?

I have a similar problem with your automobile ownership. Why do you want to own the vehicle's cumbersome structure with its bumpers, engine, drive train, and wheels? Isn't it just the interior that you want to feel is your portable home? And why own rather than rent the vehicle, especially when it's idle 90 percent of the time? And why exchange it for a new one every four years? It's as if this "system" has some purpose other than transportation. What am I missing?

Well, the basic purpose is reliable transportation, but since that's available from several competing products, the secondary purposes become pivotal in this hotly contested marketplace. Acquiring a new auto every four years has to do with style differentiation which you probably relate to our caveman legacy or some symbolic interpretations. Then, as with everything else, evolving technology impacts our auto performance and maintenance. In particular, trained mechanics and replacement parts are increasingly displaced by diagnostic computers specifying which assembly to replace, rather than identifying and replacing the defective part. Repair of older cars is accordingly more problematic with uncertain availability of qualified mechanics and replacement parts. If the car owner can tolerate this uncertainty and has no interest in communicating symbolic styling messages to adjacent drivers by means of the auto's appearance, well, then I suppose transportation costs could be reduced substantially.

I'm sure you also have a logical answer as to why each vehicle carries its own engine, fuel supply, braking, and steering subsystems rather than merely coupling the passenger container to an overhead conveyor system.

It's a bit complicated. Early autos evolved carrying all that functionality because braking, gear shifting, and steering required the driver's mechanical energy. Separating the passenger compartment wouldn't have been a simple electrical plug-socket decoupling in those days. And initially, there wasn't enough traffic to justify costs of a conveyor system. Then, by the time there *was* sufficient auto traffic, the right-of-way costs of real estate intervened. In addition, powerful auto, fuel, trucking, and insurance industries were eager to keep things basically the same.

That explanation seems to parallel your explanation of why your airplanes haul all those ludicrous takeoff and landing subsystems around.

I'd not made that connection, but yes, I think so. Technologies for improving performance of vehicles, auto, train, ship and aircraft; they all look promising until we examine the cost of upgrading the required infrastructures. As we've already discussed, starting from scratch today, we'd probably design aircraft with adaptive rather than rigid wing surfaces and maybe shock-absorbing, contoured runways rather than our passive, lengthy, linear ones. Rather than installed aboard each aircraft, we probably could design ground-based launch-landing control and energy recycling mechanisms all runway-imbedded. I'm sure we could do all that.

Yes! Why not now?

The front-end capital and institutional costs of airline industry conversion would be prohibitive and not compatible with pre-existing systems. There's always a better technology available which offers major improvements. But the economic or institutional or marketing and distribution costs of conversion are substantial barriers, especially when including the vagaries of political turf wars and changing consumer predilections. The same comments pertain to auto and bus systems.

But that doesn't seem to be happening with your cell phones, for example. The market and product upgrades seem to have taken off very quickly and to have assimilated new technologies almost effortlessly.

True. And not only because the actual value and costs of cell phones are so much improved over traditional phones. It's also because we can inject cell phone systems gradually and compatibly to accommodate new applications and markets profitably without replacing pre-existing products or their infrastructures. There was no need for major capital or institutional disruption as prerequisite to getting cell phone systems started and growing. In that sense it was easier than opening a restaurant. Also, companies weren't burdened with the heavy, exploitative hand of insurance carriers since health and safety are secondary considerations.

I see.

Incidentally, I'm delighted at your observations. Your perspective as an extraterrestrial spawns these inquiries. But most of us growing up with autos and airplanes as they've always been; we don't think to raise such questions. We Earthlings are seldom taught to think about the vehicle as a system, examining its life cycle, stakeholders and subsystems; the very systems aspects we've been discussing.

Thank you for the compliment. My less gracious observation is that if this profligate waste of resources and idle technologies, of economic and human capital, could somehow be redirected to bring the civilizations of your adversaries and yourselves together, little would be lost among your affluent citizens and much might be gained in fairness and stability on this planet.

I'm looking forward to our dinner meeting.

I'm recognizing that although you can't make the proverbial horse drink the water you've led him to, that's not so with you humans! Oblivious to realistic cost-value-satisfaction levels, consumer purchasing decisions seem largely shaped not by self-interest but by social pressures, tradition, and crowd-following patterns. But if properly managed the enormous economic distortions of government regulation and subsidies could probably fund remedial initiatives with negligible hardship. Maybe just a touch of consumer education here and there could trigger an avalanche, and not just in the marketplace of products but also in your policies and politics.

Our regular chat room schedule tomorrow?

Yes!

SESSION 13

I think I'm ready to continue our conversation about counterterrorism and Iraq. Maybe we can finish it.

*Good. I've been continuing a bit of research on my own. Within
your government, there had to be systems and people solely concerned with counterterrorism; not interested in oil, politics, or constituency loyalties. It still smells like a conspiracy to me. Look at all
the money, lives, goodwill, and resources squandered. How come? I
still don't understand.*

Primarily, a correct set of concepts were needed. If I was
tasked to develop a counterterrorism system, I'd first be sure I
understood the anatomy of terrorism, the principle categories,
what it is and what it isn't, how it works, how it grows and
evolves, how it is countered, and how it atrophies. This would
include terrorisms' interactions at the grass roots, community,
state, and global levels. I'd also need to understand its context:
sociopolitical, technological, philosophical, and cultural. I'd try
to know these things' past, present, and future. Given the complexity and dynamism of terrorism, I'd also recognize an ongoing need to constantly improve my understandings and

knowledge; the specific intelligence as well as the conceptual. I'd correlate all this with counterterrorism mechanisms to understand what works and doesn't work.

Wouldn't they have done that, too? What sort of different insights would you expect to get?

Well, I can only speculate but there seem to be several insights that apparently haven't affected high-level decisions or behaviors. The prominence and importance of counterterrorism is unprecedented militarily, economically, socio-politically, and culturally. Consequently, acquiring budgets, public, and executive attention is all greatly facilitated if related to fighting terrorism. But to really optimize strategy and programs calls for a broader, more selective and diverse set of initiatives. For example, regional programs to develop community institutions might be cost-effective in expunging or insulating terrorism.

That seems logical. But browsing through my "English for Extraterrestrials" suggests that terror is a response to attack. It is multifaceted in that the terrorist's attack could be focused via snipers, or diffused via car bombs, intended for civilian or military personnel, property, or infrastructure, conveyed by a suicide bomber or missile-launching submarine. The terror attack's purpose might be to reduce capability or will to fight or support for other fighters or to pressure governments. The terror itself could be intensified by vivid TV broadcasts or mitigated by portrayal of the "terrorists" as liberators or freedom-fighter insurgents. So isn't "terrorist" an ambiguous, confusing term?

Certainly, but get used to that. I don't know how it is on your planet but here on Earth we often mislabel a condition or cause with terminology which literally describes the result or symptom. I suppose that's to get people more activated but it often masks the appropriate remedy.

I'm not sure I understand what you are saying.

OK. We often don't label a problem or condition or disease as such, but rather as its manifestation.

What?

For example; labeling a "disease" as osteoporosis meaning porous bones or emphysema meaning swollen lung tissue; that will send us to the pharmacy. But these *symptoms* most probably have been caused by a sedentary lifestyle, so should probably send us to a gymnasium. In economics, we meticulously monitor and apply policies keyed to control "inflation" or "unemployment". Aside from their seriously flawed derivations, such indices are actually symptoms or manifestations of underlying policies which deserve our proactive attention.

So as you suggest, the cause of "terrorism" is indeed multifaceted and heterogeneous. The term is good for gaining attention, program support or news releases. The term is not good for the refined delineation necessary for designing the tools, programs, or strategies to actually deal with the problems. Thus, to say we are engaged in a global war against terrorism is not very helpful except to terrorist groups who might not have thought of networking together.

That's fascinating and quite important. OK, another question: Terrorism in the dictionary sense seems to have been around throughout your history. Are there any new elements?

Yes, there certainly are. The damage that can be inflicted and reported instantly and globally is unprecedented. Perpetrators' organizational invisibility, mobility, logistics, training, and modern weaponry present a greatly intensified threat. This threat is not surprising to those who have been watching these trends over the years. The organizational units are small, loosely coupled, and well-funded by oil and drug money. As they hear

American leaders claim they are interconnected, they become interconnecting. As American experts explain and leaders decry our vulnerabilities, they learn of our vulnerabilities. As we emphasize our differences in culture, socioeconomics, and religion, the perpetrators' zeal and recruiting is enhanced and the conviction grows that they are under attack and must prevail or die.

This all sound rather amazing and very relevant to my visit. Your situation appears to be a radically new challenge, yet the elements don't all seem so new and different. Why is that?

Excellent comment and question! Maybe you *are* from an advanced civilization. ☺.

If something is new, people pay more attention. Our leaders, who are always chasing "market share," know that. Also, if a threat or opportunity has not been addressed and resolved, that deficiency is more acceptable if it is "new" rather than something that's been around and is still unresolved. So you're entitled to some confusion as to what's new and what isn't.

I know you well enough by now to know you'd probably like examples:

- The availability of potent weapons and the global networking of people, information and funds; that's all new. Simply killing more of them than us no longer assures victory.

- Disparities in health, welfare, justice, opportunity, and culture, while not new, have become vividly evident to all, along with newly available mechanisms for change. Leaders' policies and pronouncements have new impact.

- The political and socioeconomic impacts of refugee policies have greatly intensified as their hardships have become vividly evident in the media. That's new.

- Successful counterterrorism must include grass-roots combat and its supportive intelligence. The terrorists and their collaborators, families, and communities must be persuaded to reject their fellow combatants or at least to stop supporting them. This makes "blunt" initiatives such as carpet-bombing, sanctuary, and infrastructure destruction, land mines, and martial law largely counterproductive. The collateral damage and empathy produced is substantial relative to damage inflicted on the perpetrators, given their mobility and virtual invisibility.

- Utilization of suicide warriors is not new. Despite advances in the technologies of fuses and remote control mechanisms, the increased use of suicide bombers, while not new, per se, has intensified owing to the emotions evoked, shaped, and amplified by the media. That's new.

- Denigrating other religions and ethnicity isn't new. It is necessary to feel righteous about one's cause and gratifying to perceive the enemy as subhuman and evil. But if you want his soldiers to defect or his leadership to seek peace, that perception had best be muted, maybe even reconsidered, in light of subsequent "nation building" challenges.

- Intensifying, often reinterpreting religion has always been an especially potent element for fighters from an impoverished background. Their opponents' affluence engenders the necessary righteousness, dehumanization, and antagonism necessary for combat. Without property, self-confidence, or much self-worth, the belief that one is fighting for some larger-than-self ideal has always been important.

- Historically, terrorist leaders are bought off or destroyed, and their organizational components kept isolated so that small groups or cells can be individually dealt with by carrot or stick. New but probably temporary is the mass dissemination of rhetoric intended to intimidate terrorists, disparage their leaders and/or reassure their opponents. In today's global environment that mostly helps unify terrorist organizations, expanding and inflaming their membership.

- The historic Cold War's strategic doctrine, weapon systems and proponents are not new. But they must give way to the new realities, both threats and opportunities.

So how would you use such insights?

I'd use them with others to maintain and sharpen the focus on five distinct objectives:

1. Identify and combat the proximate terrorist threats, any gang and warlord affiliations, and support elements. It is vital to differentiate mercenaries from dedicated reformers and actual enemies from their "vassal" states. Although terrorism has the same impact on its victims regardless of its source, perpetrators differ from one another substantially. Counterterrorism initiatives should be focused and customized, avoiding terrorists-alliance responses. Divide and conquer still works!

2. Build and apply various prevention capabilities. Confront economic, sociopolitical, and cultural situations which are collateral "amplifiers" of terrorism.

3. Establish vigorous, enlightened programs for winning hearts and minds of potential or switchable terrorists, their families, leaders, and communities. Establish mutual understanding, interests, and respect via wide-ranging collaborative undertakings.

4. Since globalization precludes performing initiatives 1, 2, and 3 alone, reworking and constantly upgrading intergovernmental alliances, treaties, agreements, and public relations would be required. Beyond mere collaboration is the necessity for partially relinquishing governments' control selectively within their alliances. This would especially relate to sanctions, intelligence, WMD control, disarming militias, and genocide enthusiasts.

5. In this politically and emotionally charged arena, maintain strategic goals, paths, and initiatives that are relevant and realistic. Accept that "terrorism" as a set of combat tactics, can be limited but probably not eradicated. Thanks to modern communication and weapons, it is sustained and exacerbated by the rich-poor gap plus tribal, ethnic, and religion animosities. Only combating the terrorists de jour may be satisfying and necessary but not sufficient.

Well, isn't that all sort of self-evident? Why didn't your leaders do all that?

Apparently they focused almost entirely on the first of the five without the sort of organized analysis and testing that a high-level systems approach could have provided. Moreover, leaders also need to get the subsystems' inputs and outputs right. Otherwise, the result is "unintended consequences," which is what happened, owing to the aforementioned absence of relevantly educated, experienced people at the top. And lest we forget, counterterrorism was only the stated priority.

Finally, such a five-fold strategy wouldn't have been very popular at home as the cacophony of hawks shouting "Sissies!" and doves shouting "Human rights violators!" would attest. Besides, a flamboyant attack and/or public denigration of a few fragile governments of reluctant allies would play much better on the home front despite lost participation of their intelligence and diplomacy networks. And from Vietnam, we learned that home-front support is essential.

Why didn't the other governmental elements step in?

Good question. America's laudatory checks-and-balance system was in check and out of balance as the White House team expertly orchestrated the domestic scene, providing sufficient fear to maintain unquestioned loyalty and sufficient reassurances to maintain economic stability.

Then to maintain harmony across the governmental spectrum, the Homeland Security Agency was formed by rearranging and integrating disparate counterterrorism organizations in the myriad of government agencies; except for the most important ones, not because this was the best way to really pursue homeland security, but because it was a smart, simple way to harmonize pre-existing political fiefdoms of counterterrorism And lest we forget, this all was happening immediately after 9/11, with everyone waiting for the second shoe to fall. We knew enough to be scared but not enough to know how scared we should be, of whom and what to do about it. A few mistakes are certainly understandable in retrospect. So I don't need your super-spy theory to explain what happened.

If leadership was as bad as you indicate, why have there been no further 9/11s here in America? Doesn't that indicate they've been doing things about right?

Well, to quote my favorite musicologist, I'm no expert, although I start to feel like one when I hear others speculating on this very important question. But I suspect that our opponents have recognized that in our dealing with fears of more 9/11s, our self-inflicted wounds continue to exceed whatever damage our adversaries might cause us. Or maybe the terrorists' suppliers and mentors don't want to upset the U.S. economy, which would jeopardize their investment portfolios and oil markets. But like I say, I'm no expert.

Are you also saying that if systems engineers ran the world, it might survive?

Not really. I'm only saying that a handy tool for demystifying a paradox is to map the stakeholders and system elements. Next, identifying the input initiatives, performing an analysis of the probable outputs; at minimum, this will facilitate debate, analysis, and avoidance of unintended consequences. Particularly when the details are both important and changing, a systems approach, coupled with full knowledge of the crucial input/output relationships, can augment the fearless leaders' intuition and charm.

Good answer from a systems engineer. Now as a management consultant, what would be your primary recommendation?

I'd need more in depth information and knowledge of the current and projected situation, of course. But I'd probably recommend forming a Department of Counterterrorism, distinct from the Defense Department, with its own cabinet secretary.

How would that differ from your Department of Homeland Security?

The DHS has a different purpose and systems aggregation level. Its intent seems to be for public relations, that is, to demonstrate purposeful action to and coordinate communication with domestic publics. Counterterrorism's threats, alliances, weapons, and combat prerogatives have become global.

Then why not put it in the Pentagon? As I understand it, historically, your navy and army were separate but coordinated in order to fight two distinct kinds of wars. That worked well and subsequently your air force was created to fight its new kind of war, yet coordinated with the army and navy. Now terrorism presents the next radically new kind of war which also requires coordination with the pre-existing armed services. So why not include counterterrorism as part of your Defense Department?

Yes, that's logical. But of even greater importance is counterterrorism's intrinsic linkage to the other departments: State and Justice, even Commerce and Treasury. Therefore, to minimize bureaucratic resistance, turf, and budget negotiations, it should be separate from but coordinated with the Defense Department. It's all about the subsystems' versus system's level of aggregation and stakeholders thereof.

That's very interesting and illuminating. I think you are really starting to zero in on specifics, and I think it's about time for me to leave. You've got a good grip on the conceptual issues. Implementation now becomes the challenge and you're the systems expert. Besides, I have obligations at home.

Are you serious? We're just beginning to put some flesh on the bones here. I don't think I can do anything without your continuing help. You must know that. Is there some other reason for leaving?

Well, since you asked, I'm actually being called back. I haven't wanted to mention it, but my people feel I've gone far beyond the guidelines and ground rules of my mission here. They require me to return immediately.

I don't understand.

They apparently feel that I've become too involved with ... with everything here. It's complicated, but I must return immediately.

Look, we're late for our dinner meeting. Let's talk about it at the restaurant. You owe me—us, that much. Promise?

All right.

Session 14

So what happened to our restaurant meeting? I sat at the bar for half an hour before I got your message from the maitre de that you'd had to cancel at the last minute. A serious emergency? Maybe a long distance phone call from home? What happened?

I'm very sorry. I do apologize and I'll tell you about it later. Everything is all right and thanks for asking. Maybe we can reschedule?

Sure. As it turned out the evening wasn't a failure at all as far as I was concerned. While sitting at the bar, I got into conversation with the most entrancing woman—great body. Anyway, let's reschedule. How's next Monday?

Well, maybe. But first tell me about this woman. What did you discuss?

Frankly, I don't recall much of the conversation. It may have been about the football game everyone was watching on TV—it was Monday night, you'll recall. But all I could think of was taking her to bed.

Is that really all you Earthlings can ever think about? No wonder this place is so, so ... words fail me.

Look, don't be so judgmental. And for your edification, I haven't had this kind of a first-meeting reaction since I was nineteen. It's just that she's so exceptional. Where were we?

We were about to reschedule, if it doesn't interfere with your romance. When are you seeing her again?

I don't know, so actually I would like to hold off for a bit. It's sort of odd. She wouldn't give me her name or number, so I don't know when I'm seeing her again.

Hmm, maybe she's married and you'll never see her again.

Not possible. I looked into her eyes ... not possible.

Well, maybe she's a football fan like you and you'll see her at the bar again next Monday night.

Whenever. I just know it'll happen and soon.

Good luck. Let's get on with our work.

OK. Does that mean you've decided to delay your departure?

They won't like it, but yes, I think I can justify a slightly less-precipitous exit, at least until our long-awaited dinner meeting.

Great! You intended to look at our ground transportation as counterpoint to your examining our air transport systems. Have you gotten to it yet?

Yes, and I was intrigued to see that you still use lots of passenger trains. We gave up on them quite a while ago. It was actually long ago so I may have some details wrong. But for us, the economics just didn't work, once we had alternatives. The cost of a secure, reliable, high-speed, smooth, accessible network of tracks proved prohibitive.

One problem is that proximity to population-dense markets makes for exorbitant rights-of-way, yet without proximate population, there is no market. Only when developed synchronously with new communities and accompanied by tax or regulatory disincentives penalizing alternatives were we able to produce financially viable railroad systems.

We're in the same situation, I believe. Even before we encountered security issues, we couldn't make the economics work. Another conundrum is the design itself. Tradeoffs among fuel costs, rolling stock, and track wear, plus passenger comfort and travel time are all captive to the nonsense of stopping and starting the entire train for entry/egress of 1 percent of the payload. Any vehicle's propulsion and control in its cruising mode should be quite different from its accelerating/decelerating mode. That's just simple physics.

The train stations must be closely spaced. Otherwise upon disembarking, a second, local train is required for proximity to final destinations. And of course, if the traffic isn't clustered along the right-of-way, one or several parallel tracks with lateral links are required. So the entire mess gets relocated underground—along with any hope of economic viability.

Of course at home we avoid the right-of-way costs and start-stop design problems simply by means of our overhead, high-speed gondolas that engage or disengage individual passenger capsules with individually powered vehicles for short-range personal travel, seamlessly available at passenger terminals. You've gotten as far as ski gondolas and golf carts here, but you haven't connected those two concepts for urban mass transit. As you have reminded me, the limited expertise with materials and energy storage/conversion must be the culprits, made worse perhaps by vested interests in infrastructure and real estate.

As an earthbound engineer, I agree with you. Have you examined our truck-auto modalities?

I've not gotten to trucks. I'm still dealing with amazement at your autos. I know we've talked about this before, but I still don't get it. Please help me understand it.

Sure. What's your problem?

Well, here, I'll email you my notes. Tell me what you think.

NOTES: These Earthlings insist on owning private autos whose acquisition and operating costs total perhaps 25 percent of a worker's salary; maybe 50 percent if subsidies and tax relief for highways, fuel, and superfluous insurance are included. Inexpensive vehicles designed for low maintenance and functional styling don't attract buyers. The vehicles require costly networks of roads that impose obscene ecological and safety burdens. In addition, urban congestion and pollution are toxic. The resulting suburban sprawl causes local governance to be haphazard, making employment, community life, schools, and crime control more difficult.

There are less-visible problems as well. Their very young children can't run free for safety reasons. Parents then feel compelled to impose rules that make the children feel vulnerable and incarcerated, which is bad for their early psychological development and parental relationship. A parent or child-care person must be vigilantly on duty at all times, including the time spent in autos. These childcare hours are gradually displaced by hours spent in parental chauffeuring of children to distant friends, lessons, or enrichment programs. Thus, children are shielded from self-reliance and self-discovery. Later, these vehicles provide privacy for teenagers to experiment unobserved with whatever, until licensed to drive, creating yet another set of safety concerns as well as additional parent-child tensions.

These autos befoul the air—also relations with oil producing nations, and block opportunities to develop far more efficient modes of transportation. It may relate to some weird psychic gratification rather than transportation. For example:

- *Legacies of the caveman or refugee make the option of instant mobility intensely powerful. Perhaps car owners are still trying to escape from claustrophobic shelters, predators, and weather, or are still trying to capture food or a woman.*

- *Pride of ownership is noticeably important here; mere possession hardly counts. Renting as needed is disparaged even though the owned vehicle is idle typically 90 percent of the time.*

- *Various self-denials required for employment, military service, parenting, husbanding, and compliance with laws and taboos leave the male thirsting for power, identity, and freedom— expressed vicariously via the auto's excessive engine power, body styling, and interior decor. Ungainly, expensive off-road vehicles are almost never taken off-road, but the option somehow gratifies the owner with a sense of power and freedom.*

- *Nostalgia also seems important: foot pedals, a steering wheel, and useless dashboard information are retained from early autos, when these accoutrements were needed.*

- *Incredibly, their designers, drivers, and passengers consistently resist proven safety devices: seat belts, air bags, helmets, protective rather than decorative bumpers. Even granting Earthlings' chronic denial of their mortality and vulnerability, their autos seem intended for psychic rather than transportation trips. Are Earthlings really children just playing with very expensive toys? END OF NOTES*

Yes, I can certainly help you to understand. There are benefits to mobility and psychological gratifications of owning a late model car. The combination of private auto and cell phone impart unprecedented space and time spontaneity. Mobility provides wider employment alternatives. Local government services feel the pressure to maintain quality or risk migration, hence lost votes, tax base, and real estate appreciation. Retail businesses and their customers can benefit in product range and prices via economies of scale resulting from access to a larger customer base. Similar benefits result in recreation and self-improvement options resulting from time saved and the greater distances conveniently accessible. A wider range of friends, preservation of cultural roots, range, and choice of potential spouses, houses, and such, are all facilitated by this mobility. On balance, it may be worthwhile after all.

But if the affluent countries continue clinging to traditional housing, urban configurations, and transportation, people will increasingly be working long hours at low pay. Wealth will increasingly be diverted to those who may or may not want to emulate you but will certainly want to destroy you. You seem to be providing the wealth, technology, information, and motivation for them to do so—not to mention global warming and toxic pollution. It's no wonder your leaders, even the competent ones, find it difficult to govern these days.

Well, perhaps.

I keep wondering how I can explain things to my people when I get home. Your situation is so bizarre; it must be incredible to any thoughtful, objective outsider. It occurred to me that maybe your people just don't get the necessary information to deal rationally with their reality. Maybe I should walk around a bit to learn more about your information technologies.

Yes, why don't you do that? I'll just sit here and mumble a few incantations, maybe beat on the ground with a stick.

What are you talking about?

After all, I'm just from this primitive little planet that's totally anachronistic and disorganized.

Look, I don't mind your being angry but, please don't let it interfere with our work. Same time tomorrow?

Fine for tomorrow. Have fun walking around. Among other things, I hope you discover that a touch of humility can lubricate your interviews as well as your understanding and acceptance of information, at least on this backward planet.

SESSION 15

Reviewing our last session, I'm sorry if I offended you. But there isn't time for these sensitivities.

I agree, and I apologize also. We were very much in tune during yesterday's session on transportation before I flipped out. I guess it's hard for me to accept your being from a more advanced civilization when we seem to be working in such harmony as colleagues most of the time.

I have the same problem. We are more advanced than you Earthlings in vital respects and yet I'm learning, and growing, in our collaboration. So here; I'll email you my notes on information technology. Tell me what you think.

NOTES: Earthlings have just come through some major information technology advances in computing and networking, user interfaces, and telecommunication, both carrying capacities and utilization techniques. Much recent effort and computer capacity has been devoted to the aesthetics of graphics and the illusion of versatility, making the software packages appear more "user-friendly" rather than making them more useful. Computer engineers will undoubtedly continue improvements in computing and communi-

cation, but the current dominant bottlenecks in user interfaces must be addressed. It's a bit hilarious to watch Earthlings struggling to use this suddenly available, semi-impenetrable information power while it changes faster than they can learn to apply and pay for it. It's even funnier knowing that it's temporary.

What I mean by "temporary" is that as information technology advances, the high-low range of computing power options expands from the largest supercomputers to palm-held devices, permitting large-scale economies for mass markets, such as education and entertainment. Subsequently, intervening services can be made so effective that the presence of massive computing and telecommunication becomes invisible to the end-user. At the other extreme, a smart chip, subcutaneous, or wallet-sized will be used for personal security, accessing office or garage, navigation, shopping, health monitoring, and messaging. And owners will be as oblivious to their information technologies making it all possible as today they are oblivious to the electricity running their many appliances.

But at the moment, unsophisticated home users must struggle in actually using their various computerized devices. Help desks intended to mitigate the struggle are revealing. First comes the endlessly repeated phone message: "Your call is very important to us," eventually followed by "This call is being recorded for training purposes," followed by "My name is Joe," ending eventually with "We're here 24/7 to solve your problem." I suppose that providing four misstatements in a single transcontinental phone call is indicative of rather advanced telecommunications after all.

So there is much work to be done. Operator interfaces are somewhat archaic in my planet's terms, particularly the highly standardized keyboard without tactile or eye-movement augmentation. Here, visual displays are still two dimensional and lack even flicker or texture modulation. For some important applications, like weather and earthquake prediction, econometric and sociopolitical models, satellite photography, intelligence analyses, and health care, selecting from the limitless data for computer processing and display are the remaining bottlenecks. Knowing what to look at and knowing what it means is the problem, now that hardware and software have become so advanced. Also, engineers haven't yet developed sophisticated speech, olfactory, or tactile linkages. They need implants or genetic modifications for telepathic or perceptual amplification. Earthlings seem to have a taboo against implants or genetic modification, even for their astronauts—imagine how that must burden life support and safety systems for long voyages!

Earthlings are grappling with what they lyrically call their "Information Revolution." Unfortunately, this revolution has used very little science: some bits of theoretical mathematics; numerical analysis, information theory for communication, database structures, that sort of thing. But most of the information-related science has been in support of developing the building blocks; the hardware and software components for computing and communication. Some science has been almost grudgingly conducted as needed for applications, such as artificial intelligence, systems simulation, epistemology for cryptography, and language translation. The intersections of information and nano-science are promising for computing, genome, and brain research as examples.

While the information revolution here has first impacted the affluent privileged classes and is trickling down, as happens with all revolutions, this revolution, unlike the others, ultimately permeates and radically affects all classes. While aggregate productivity increases are already substantial, the promise of reduced socioeconomic gaps via information technologies; that promise may never be fulfilled.

I suppose my engineering colleague would relate it to the system aggregation level. The airline pilot is confronted with displays and functional options, truly remarkable for human ergonomics. Then, to keep him and his passengers alive and successfully reaching their destinations requires an army of support people fitted out with voluminous standards and procedures manuals, navigation and communication nets, air traffic and ground traffic controllers; even mechanics who actually know what to do when the pilot reports a flashing console light. I find that just a little amusing, if not amazing.

They're at a similar stage with other information systems. Earthlings are remarkably versatile intellectually and ergonomically. So they design and provide versatile software and its continuous upgrades, which keep the harried computer operator in a learning mode and calling for help for any non-routine situation, choosing from a large set of semi-available, semi-competent help desk personnel. Of those, only a few are qualified to put the troubled operator in touch with someone who can actually help the situation. It seems quite similar to the aircraft cockpit philosophy of loading the pilot with more information access than he/she knows what to do with even in trouble-free modes. And when trouble strikes? Calls for help are discouraged by delay and responders of marginal competence. Incidentally, they seem to do the same thing with your lawyers, teachers, and doctors. END OF NOTES

Look, the computing power which presently fits in my shirt pocket barely fit into a building a few decades ago. Give me a break! I can't tell if your condescension is just part of your makeup or if you genuinely feel that what I see as remarkable progress, you see as trivial and inadequate. What would you have us do differently, my prince of arrogance?

Please excuse me, and thanks for the reminder. I'm used to certain levels of—never mind. To answer your question, as you have already done with factories and kitchens, you should automate functions sensibly with dedicated computer control centralized to the "machine" where needed. That is, don't overload and infuriate the operator or buyer just because you know how to immerse him/her in a sea of marginally useful feature, especially if the lifeguard is just learning to swim.

Your pride in applying advance information technologies quickly and mindlessly as the marketplace invites is understandable; but get over it. You are spewing information all over the landscape like untreated sewage. That can either kill your planet or be the catalyst for education and insights to advance and perhaps even save your civilization depending on how you do it. You've got to figure it out!

SESSION 16

Your walking around is producing some interesting ideas. I confess to difficulty in absorbing them, in part, I think, because of feeling distracted. It's as if you haven't quite told me why you're really here, or quite who or what you really are. Do you care to comment?

I'm impressed! You are more perceptive than I'd expected. You may be quite different from the other Earthlings I've encountered—but then maybe I'm different from other ETs you've encountered. There, my first attempt at Earthly humor!

In any case, as I'd mentioned at the outset, of all the many little planets constantly being born, maturing, and then dying of natural causes, your planet seems to be unique. My colleagues and I were somewhat incredulous, after laughing and joking about it before they sent me here. As best we can tell, instead of run-amok biology or running out of resources, your planet seems to simply be mismanaged. Our guess was that you are self-destructing from lack of knowledge. And because of that initial orientation, well, that's probably why you detect my occasional air of superiority. I'll try to be more careful from now on.

You've told me all that before. Is there something else?

Yes, there is. Of the countless small planets we study, this one is uniquely similar to ours, almost a clone but from a more primitive era. I think that as a result, I'm been feeling a camaraderie, almost a kinship and a desire to help rather than merely observe. And I find that kinship extending particularly to you personally, which is a bit disconcerting. It's interfering with the substantive work and how I'm processing my findings. I have the feeling that this will all smooth out when we meet, so let me know when you've finished fantasizing over your mystery woman and we'll schedule something.

Thank you for telling me. I have similar feelings, a bit strange since our only communication is via e-mail and in our "chat room." I increasingly have moments when I imagine us getting together, kicking back over a six-pack, watching the Lakers or some football. Strange …

Following your suggestion, I'm going to my restaurant Monday night to watch the game and look for my "mystery woman." I'll keep you posted—oops, I almost forgot. How's your "walking around" been working? Any new insights?

I rather think so, but check it out. I've been trying to take a closer look at what makes Earthlings tick; how they behave in relating themselves to survival in their environments. Then I looked at how they cluster: relationships, family, community, and state and non-state organizations. I am especially interested in how they communicate and how the leadership functions.

So what else have you learned about us Earthlings? Tell me more about your random walks in our forest.

Not random and it's more jungle than forest. There is such total concentration on sex, violence, and power. At first, I couldn't understand where that comes from and then, how Earthlings have time or energy to accomplish anything unrelated to sex, violence, and power. It permeates everything from design of your automobiles and movies to your art, your religions, everything. Some of it must be residual legacies from prehistoric days. I wanted to shout "Come on hunters-gatherers-warriors, enough already! Get real. There's enough time and resources out there to fix your own mess." It must be very arduous for primitives to adjust to modernity—lots of contradictions to control.

How so?

Well, there's this caveman versus modern man dichotomy. There's the yearning for freedom, mobility, the independent self with personal integrity versus having to relinquish some integrity and autonomy in order to affiliate with one or more societal entities or even with one's reflected self-image. Many of you feel alone, abandoned, and needy for a greater sense of affiliation. You combat an underlying sense of vulnerability by acting as if immortal. You maintain a sense of superiority to others, a pet dog if no humans suffice. You talk about and sometimes perform selfless, ethical acts. Is that a bribe, leaving something of value behind for the ominous distant future, or is it to justify past behaviors or to bolster a weak self-image?

Interesting, not just what you've observed about us humans but also what you're saying about yourself. I'm really looking forward to our meeting. What else have you discovered?

I don't understand that comment, but maybe when we get together. What else have I discovered? Your leaders are a joke. In particular:

- *To get power, they must suppress their true identity—self-emasculation in a sense. Then, once successful, they revert to counterproductive acts of sex, violence, and aggression to restore their sense of self and power. How childish!*

- *To retain power they frighten their constituency with external demons, preferably live ones; they rattle sabers, lead cheers, slay a few dragons, but not all, and this nonsense somehow endears them to their primitive constituents.*

- *Leaders lie adeptly and persuasively, with charm and warmth. How do they accomplish that? Is it training, or are they unaware when they are doing it?*

- *In conflict resolution they select from among the standard tactics: intimidation, concealment, dissembling, direct combat, end runs. Too often the selection seems based on what's worked before, or what feels comfortable or is a momentary crowd-pleaser. That might explain intimidation's durability. It should be obvious, but apparently isn't, that you can no longer intimidate an enemy who has become able to retaliate and hide.*

- *Some of these leadership deficiencies probably result from the almost casual rituals for selecting leaders. In your open democracies, public-sector leaders are picked, packaged, and sold to voters much like consumer products. But your planet is in an epoch where leadership is crucial. America's Cold War victory over the USSR, erroneously attributed to the superiority of capitalism over socialism, actually resulted from the inferiority—although not by much, of the USSR's leader selection process.*

Is it all bad news?

No. Resiliency, creativity, determination, capacity to grow and evolve—these attributes of Earthlings I'd rate superior to our own. I suppose the relatively inhospitable, semi-harsh ecology has forced these attributes to the fore here. But these same traits perpetuate, for example, your steadfast retention of outmoded partitioning and seg-regating.

Off you go again. What are you talking about?

Sorry. This is only an example, but an important one. You dis-connect and segregate education, recreation, and work. Then you encapsulate each in specifically designated organizations, times, and locations. It's crazy. You even separate learning from working, not realizing that work is mostly learning how or what to do and that actually doing the work then yields the vital insight of what to learn next. On our planet, if the task consists only of doing work, we rele-gate it to robots.

Specialize and segregate. Perhaps it's all part of an evolutionary legacy, formed in a time when parents admonished their children with "Don't stop to play when being chased by dinosaur," or "I'll teach you how to make fire, but only after you clean your cave." Appropriate segregation is vital; otherwise it can be dangerous, costly, and ludicrous in today's world.

But that seems to be your pattern—even at the most intimate interpersonal level. The female's anatomical zone of sexual stimula-tion is located several inches away from the male's and her moment of climax, if at all, seldom coincides with her partner's—evolution-ary legacy, perhaps, but yet another example of Earthlings' parti-tion-segregate behavior. Even when those moments of intimacy include integrative bonding there follows a quick retreat to privacy; sleep or separated activities: tinkering in the kitchen or garage or office.

OK, so granted, we segregate. But then we make adjust-ments.

Exactly! I have another little list of your "adjustments:"

- *Your private/public sector separation is sharp and unambiguous in concept, but then private-sector special-interests drive the public sector's legislation and election results. Your private corporations, specifically chartered to make money without breaking laws, are then pressured to be "good citizens." What's that about?*

- *Each of the federal agencies is designated to both regulate and protect their constituents. The Federal Aviation Administration regulates safety, yet supports the airline industry. The Department of Agriculture regulates and inspects agricultural products, yet fosters agriculture technologies and farm subsidies. The Energy Department regulates energy production and distribution firms while sponsoring research and lobbying for legislation supportive of the energy industries.*

- *Global issues of world peace, WMD, integrity of information systems, pandemics, and genocide are not addressed globally but by each country. Consequently, ad hoc coalitions of these countries form agencies which generate unenforceable, often ignored treaties and resolutions.*

- *State governments do very little at the state level. Mostly, they grapple with regional issues on the one hand and very local issues on the other.*

- *Only a small fraction of military personnel have combat roles. Homeland security is assigned to civilian agencies.*

- *Your Defense Department is neatly organized according to its original combat environment; i.e. the Army fights on the ground, the Navy on and in the ocean, the Air Force in the air and space. Except that the Army has its own aircraft, amphibious, and landing craft. The Navy has its own soldiers; marines, as well as an air force including carrier aircraft, helicopters, drones, missiles, and satellites. The Air Force facilities, operations, and personnel are almost entirely ground-based. You haven't bothered to form a homeland anti-terrorism force, even though that's the newest, most dangerous, and unique combat challenge.*

Wrong! We formed the Homeland Security Department, not just another Defense Department force but rather an entire stand-alone Department.

OK, you're probably right. I get confused by the labels. Where I come from, your Defense Department would be called the War Department. Your stand-alone Homeland Security Department does appear to stand alone; a collection of disparate organizations that needed to be part of what we might call the Miscellaneous Department, but not designed to seriously address homeland security.

Got it. But frankly, you're discouraging me.

Really? Discouraged? That's interesting. I'm not. In fact, I think I'm beginning to see the path. Incidentally, thanks in part to your systems approach, I'm beginning to understand some of the many paradoxes you live with.

So tell me about "the path." How do other planets make it? Do they carefully avoid big income gaps? Is the middle class a vital socioeconomic stabilizer? What do they do about each of our four kinds of adversaries: loose cannons like Timothy McVeigh, non-government networks like al Qaeda, failed and rogue states?

These are certainly the right questions. What's the difference between "rogue" and "failed" states in your parlance?

Rogue states are states that are uncooperative, maybe even antagonistic, to our network of alliances. Some states we label as "rogue" probably don't deserve that pejorative. Failed states are states failing to care for and be cared for by their citizenry. They are probably not more fertile breeding grounds for terrorism than other states, but we tend to think so because we have more trouble collaborating with those governments in counterterrorism initiatives.

We don't have time in this session to deal with your question about the path except very generally. So for the moment, I'll just mention the obvious: when deciding where to go, it helps to know where you've been and where you are. Reducing nostalgic devotion to anachronisms will free up vast energy and resources for getting it right. So there is hope if you support leaders who want to go where the people want to go, and whose understanding, commitment, and capability will get them there. Otherwise, it'll continue to be just one paradox after another.

Your mini-lectures are starting to sound like mine.

Maybe we should both get out more.

Now that you mention it, I'm off to my regular Monday night TV at the bar. At least with football there's usually a winning side. And maybe she'll be there. Regular time tomorrow?

Absolutely. And I'll expect a full report. ☺

Session 17

Before we go further, I need to clarify something. Our "chats" are giving me insights and perspectives I'd never encountered and it's exhilarating much of the time. But then I get the feeling that you have some kind of a hidden agenda in our discussions.

And another thing: I tend to fill in the limitations of e-mail with interpretations and speculations about the other party. Somehow, I can't do that with you. I don't know what's going on here beneath the surface.

And why did you select me? You could have selected a retired prostitute and probably learned a lot more about the human condition on this planet than you can from me.

Questions, questions ... I have more than a few myself. It might help if you told me more about yourself, how you perceive your reality, and how you think about it.

Truthfully, right at this moment I don't have a very firm grip on my reality. At the time of my divorce, which was an obscenely protracted process, I became focused on decluttering my life. I gave up unnecessary furniture and other physical possessions, as well as some unrewarding, time-consuming activities and friends. I live an almost monastic life so describing it won't tell you much. I certainly don't typify most other Earthlings—especially right now.

Why right now? Does it have anything to do with your mystery lady?

Exactly. I met her again at the same bar and we actually had dinner together. So right now, my life or at least my mind is suddenly more than a little "cluttered."

And?

Well, not surprisingly, the physical attraction was undiminished; it's "over the top." But to my amazement, she has a mind, personality, and career to match. There were actually moments when having sex with her wasn't uppermost on my mind.

But why "amazement?"

Nothing special. It's just a stereotype thing, the idea that beautiful, sexy women don't have to develop a mind or persona, and therefore don't. Developing their brain and personality would just get in the way of finding a man to protect and provide for them.

Is that your perception, too? Your t-shirt date comes to mind.

Of course not! And after last night, especially so. If you don't mind, I'd rather change the subject. I'm seeing her next week and maybe my mind will be more—let's move on, please.

Certainly, however apropos of the topic, would you be interested in one of my early journal entries in which I tried to—here, I'll e-mail it. You can decide to read or discard it.

Sure send it along. I could use some entertainment or insights, intergalactic or local.

Fine, take a look and tell me what you think.

NOTES: Under a thin veneer of "civilization," males here are chronically poised to scatter their seed as broadly and often as possi-

ble. I suppose it's a caveman legacy. The more sex-obsessed, aggressive males would, as such, have fathered more children, perpetuating these traits into modern times. Only quite recently in geological time has relationship commitment been grafted onto the male psyche, as society's imperative for protective child rearing and to attract the more eligible or scarce women. The recent conversion of the male from a "range free" hunter-gatherer-warrior to a monogamous, taboo-compliant worker-gatherer evidently does not come without his feeling resentment, confusion, and ambivalence.

As for the women, living the carefree, nomadic life couldn't have been especially pleasant. Women probably didn't enjoy being gang-raped or delivering their own babies, nurturing the occasional survivor alone, and otherwise living off the land. Those that managed to attract and keep just a single male as protector had lots more surviving children than the others, so these traits and patterns persisted.

Again, from primitive times, the best protectors were those who felt ownership of what they protected; hence the popularity and perpetuation of the notion of women as property. Given the alternatives, even women must have supported that custom. And one thing led to another. As primitive man evolved, feeling ownership, power, and control wasn't enough. He also wanted to feel welcome, needed, and wanted. So did his partner. Actualization has not been easy, with marauding warriors and beasts of the jungle, work place harassment, mortgage payments, and snarling in-laws.

Self-gratification within this process probably wouldn't have even occurred to women until quite recently. The most advanced women might have begun to recognize that nature hadn't treated them fairly, demanding that she be temptress and lover, cave-keeper and farmer. Particularly while "Mr. Wonderful" sat around grunt-

ing at how she wasn't as much fun as when he'd first raped her and why had she let the fire go out of their romance and cave?

Now suddenly, in geological time, she lives beyond childbearing years, and is still angry at being torn between the several roles nature placed upon her, as is her mate. So he reverts to slightly modernized versions of traditional roles: breadwinner, TV watcher, sports enthusiast, philanderer, and boozer while she takes up tennis, grand-mothering, philandering, or book clubs. Since primitive women died young from violence, childbirth, or disease, evolution failed to prepare their immune systems for dealing with longevity; burdening them today with menopause, osteoporosis, and daughters-in-law.

Earthlings are still primitives. For example, their mating dance is remarkable. His only thought is consummation, so he says and does whatever he thinks is required. He has little genetic propensity toward "companionship" or co-parenting, the joys of which are experiential rather than instinctual. Accordingly, honest communication during the couple's early courtship is unlikely. She dresses and comports herself to preserve his interest and her independence while she considers his potential as hunter-gatherer-warrior, acceptability to the tribe and genetic makeup for potential offspring. Of secondary importance is whether he is exciting, spontaneous, and independent, yet will be nurturing, loyal, loving, and predictable, once mated.

When a mutual commitment forms, it is very hard to sustain, given the limited psychological maturity and rigid programming of the partners' early development. He often reverts to his ingrained roles of seed-scattering and hunter-gatherer-warrior, and she as mother and cave-keeper. Accumulated resources and adrenalin are then allocated to trinkets acquisition, which now include dwellings, cars, cruises, appliances. Cave people! *END OF NOTES*

Thanks! That's actually helpful and timely. Without realizing it, I guess I've exemplified your caveman trying to "fit in" to modernity. So what has me confused right now is that the non-physical appeal for my mystery woman seems comparably intense and complementary to the initial, intense physical attraction. I've never experienced that before. Strange. Please, no locker room jokes about it now.

Not at all. I thank you for being able to tell me.

So let's move on. You've mentioned observing some paradoxes recently. Maybe I can help with some of them.

I'd appreciate some help. I think I see a group of paradoxes for which there might be a generic explanation.

Your nuclear nations publicly threaten the non-nuclear nations with sanctions or pre-emptive attack if they strive to become nuclear. Of course, that provokes the non-nuclear countries' totally expectable response of striving harder to become nuclear.

- *The war on illegal drug suppliers effectively assures high prices and profits for that industry.*

- *America's anti-Castro policy has perpetuated his regime quite nicely.*

- *America encourages democracy and elections everywhere, but then denies support to the elected government if its preferred candidate loses.*

- *Efforts to control oil-producing countries induce flagrantly anti-American rhetoric and policies; with similar reactions from producers of pollution, trade barriers and "terrorism."*

And therefore?

There's a pattern. These problems seem to be created or exacer-
bated by your leaders' rhetoric and policies. That's gratifying domes-
tically, I suppose, but counterproductive in confronting the
problems. Your government's pronouncements which demonize and
threaten international actors seem to make them more focused and
resolute while consolidating their supporters. Obvious domestic ini-
tiatives that would undercut these external actors' economic or
political programs would be far less costly and risky to your citizens.
To me that's paradoxical in the extreme.

Like what "obvious initiatives?"

Well, as you keep reminding me, I'm new here. But if America
simply reduced its oil dependency slightly or became a proactive
champion of human rights or refugee relief the international impact
could be substantial. If you became more partner than chief in care-
fully selected aspects of WMD and environmental policies; those
sorts of things would seem self-evident. No? Why hasn't America's
self-interest induced such initiatives almost automatically?

I get it. Good comment. Maybe we should look at some of
these a bit more closely.

Yes. Let's consider this one: In consumer countries the illicit drug
industry diverts and consumes tremendous wealth, strains law
enforcement, corrupts government officials, and contaminates rela-
tions with supplier countries. Whereas decriminalizing and regulat-
ing product distribution would collapse the lure of its extraordinary
profitability. Rehabilitation treatment of addicts would reduce the
market, unload the criminal justice system, and improve family and
community relations.

But attacking the current sources and suppliers seems foolish.
Even when occasionally successful, the extreme profit incentive must
assure the advent of new sources and suppliers. Your so-called "war

on drugs" seems intrinsically costly, dangerous, and counterproductive.

Again, a detailed diagram of stakeholders and their linkages to the system would be useful to explicate the several factors. The drug enforcement and criminal justice organizations have program budgets and jobs to protect. The drug producers maintain pricing, marketplace, and organizational discipline by virtue of being under attack. They also have the resources to buy information and influence as needed to defend and enhance their positions.

Also, America's Calvinistic traditions are moralistic and punitive toward deviants, that is, the users. In our tradition, swift retribution and punishment are much more gratifying than rehabilitation. We also get nervous about prohibition repeal's potential for "opening the floodgates" to new addicts, despite the contrary experience of other countries. There was a time when the outcomes of rehabilitation programs and prohibition repeal were uncertain, but no longer. In essence, the stakeholders with power to change don't really want to, so there it is.

Hmm, OK. Here's another one.

Israel's historical tit-for-tat strategy for dealing with its Palestinian neighbors seems to have predictably enhanced Palestinian capabilities, resolve, and external support. It must have burdened Israel's economy, domestic cohesion, and international goodwill; serving no purpose useful for resolving matters. Wouldn't unilateral withdrawal plus "nation building" and/or major military suppression have been preferable for Israel long ago? Would a detailed stakeholder analysis help clarify the situation for me?

Well, if we included the relevant time frame and levels of detail, I think so. We'd probably see that the "tit-for-tat" policy you describe maintained domestic adherence to Israel's incumbent leadership by almost containing an active enemy. The "almost" demonstrated the enemy to be palpable and dangerous, yet containable. The policy justified maintaining a vibrant military and gave the Jewish Diaspora a sense of camaraderie and pride for a righteous, yet restrained, Israel confronting its enemies.

Other governments employ the same strategy, sometimes inadvertently. Continued violence or its threat offers hope, hence acceptance of the situation, to each side's extremist dream of ultimately destroying the other. The moderate majority stays passive, feeling powerless or fearful of escalation or retribution if it takes sides. So there's payoff to most of the various stakeholders.

Moreover consider the more extreme alternatives. For Israel, an aggressive military campaign invites portrayal of the government as a merciless bully in the international media. The alternative of "turning the other cheek" weakens factions of domestic support while strengthening the resolve and hopes of those wishing to destroy Israel.

I see what you're saying, but not quite. As an example, Israel's unilateral withdrawal from Lebanon and Gaza, leaving unemployment, corrupt governance, a legacy of violence, and no mechanism for proactively empowering the moderate factions; didn't that merely provide extremists on both sides validation and exoneration for their pre-existing positions and signal continued need for help from their respective constituencies?

Yes, but it's a confusing, multi-layered, ever-changing situation. A detailed stakeholder portrayal would probably highlight that Israel's leaders have maintained incumbency by prioritizing Israel's internal growth while defending against intermittent external enemies. The Palestinian leaders have maintained incumbency largely by blaming Israel for their people's plight, persuasively to both domestic and international audiences. Even the Palestinians' use of "suicide bombers" rather than more simple and reliable detonators helps the Israelis see their enemy as subhuman and helps the Palestinians mobilize sympathy and support for their cause.

Israeli leaders' incumbency would certainly be at risk by offering to help Palestinians' socioeconomic development. Palestinian leaders' incumbency would certainly be at risk by suddenly offering an olive branch to the Israelis. Each side's tentative overtures have been dismissed as ploys or tokenism by the other, thereby preserving the status quo of "low-intensity conflict." Digging into the details, I imagine you would find that stakeholders with the power to make significant change wouldn't believe in the merits of doing so either for themselves or constituents.

So are you saying that things will never change?

Not at all. Looking at the global system of which Israel is a subsystem provides quite a different view. Israel's direct strategic value to America ended with the Cold War. Its value as a continuing demonstration of western-style democracy for the Middle East is arguable. Israel's enemies are proliferating and collaborating, acquiring modern arms and training. Control via intimidation based on overwhelming military superiority is failing as increasingly potent and astute opponents compete in combat and in public relations via worldwide TV. You can expect that external rather than domestic issues will dominate attention of the Israeli government—and most others as well, for the period ahead.

So is it analogous to your farmer-horse situation; continuing down a path that must ultimately lead to a predictable catastrophe?

Possibly. I hope for all concerned that it'll be more like my other example of the redesign of the company-union system for negotiation. There, catastrophe was averted when powered by the stakeholders' experiencing and then recognizing their mutual vulnerabilities, then seizing the opportunities offered by high-level collaboration rather than conflict. The Middle East confrontations could play out similarly.

Incidentally, in Israel, you have an intrinsic source of paradoxes emanating from fundamental anomalies:

- Israel was formed as an equality-based democracy, yet as a Jewish state and homeland for all Jews. So how could equality work for non-Jewish Israeli citizens in a country of such limited space and natural resources?

- The neighboring governments and populations look inept, impoverished, and corrupt by comparison to Israel, a country developed with help from an energized Diaspora and populated by tough, self-actualized survivors of anti-Semitism, injustice, and poverty.

These factors accentuated by geographic proximity inhibit development of collaboration, mutual trust and friendship.

Got it. I'm still a neophyte but it seems like most of Earth's governments are inept and/or corrupt. They're increasingly unable to protect their citizens from "terrorism," from drugs and sex traffic, exploitative trade tariffs, as well as the uncontrolled flow of money, refugees, and jobs. Is this a new trend?

You're learning fast. Another paradox?

Yes. Just recently I've had an opportunity to observe one of your male Earthlings "romancing" a woman. He radiated such intensity that it was both frightening and off-putting to the woman. He says childish, patronizing things; his mating dance is ludicrous, almost insulting to her intelligence. Wouldn't it be simpler to just tell her he wants to give her his sperm and be done with it? And why does he make it so personal? At home we have—well it's a bit embarrassing to tell you, but when I first arrived here I assumed all those ATM machines scattered about were connected to an entirely different kind of bank.

This leap from international to interpersonal I find a bit breathtaking. I think I could use a break to think about—what you just said has me cogitating over the dinner I had with my mystery lady. So, same time tomorrow?

Yes, I could use a break right now, too.

Tomorrow, then.

Session 18

Let's get back to paradoxes. What about rape? I understand that only in very recent times, and in limited cultures and situations, that your women have felt sufficiently safe to say "no." But more than a third of females in this law-abiding, God-fearing country of yours are raped in their lifetimes. At least that many more must at various times want to say "no" but feel too afraid or hopeless to do so. What must that number be globally? Think of how women's behavior, mobility and feelings toward men must be constrained just in rape avoidance efforts. The costs in terms of economic and human development alone ... why do you perpetuate it? Is it that your women and children are still regarded as property and that it's the property owner's responsibility to keep his flock out of harm's way?

I'd never thought about it, but what you say sounds right. I'd guess that the rape propensity is strong, pervasive, and not easy to detect in potential perpetrators, or retroactively. But again, it would be useful to look at each major stakeholder: the victim, family, perpetrator, and the impact of rape in prisons on rehabilitation, criminal justice, and society. Then we'd examine how the stakeholders relate to the system's details, the rapist's relationship to the victim, if any, the rapist's motive, and any other facts that would produce more insight. Such analysis would provide an orderly structure from which to examine alternative anti-rape remedies systematically.

So you're probably going to tell me that alternatives are available: reinforced education, more stringent legal penalties, improved rape deterrence, and post-rape forensic devices. Such alternatives must be available now, but not promulgated. Why not?

Well, of course there are the obvious legal difficulties. The victim's reluctance to come forward, no witnesses, proving that "no" was consciously felt, expressed, and communicated, post feelings of complicity or worthlessness. It may be that at some elemental level, men still empathize with the rapist, or maybe even envy him. Certainly, many men don't perceive, think, or care about their victim's feelings, and some want them to feel overpowered as part of the act. Then too, since husbands and fathers feel protective of their wives and daughters, if rape went away, they'd have less to protect them from. Their women would feel freer to be out and about, and what might that lead to?

Well, as you say, you haven't thought about it much. So why aren't your women an organized, progressive, anti-rape force?

Good question, but why just women? I'm just a male engineer, and only very recently evolved in your view, apparently. I agree that the combination of improved forensic devices, raising the legal penalties, more privacy, sensitivity, and alacrity in data acquisition and dispute resolution all could have major impact. A carefully developed spreadsheet would probably reveal that the stakeholders with power lack the motivation. We would need to find out why and then decide how to mobilize them.

So here's a simpler yet tougher paradox. Out of self-interest, why don't the most powerful, affluent countries on Earth see the direct, palpable threat of poverty to themselves, their community, and country?

I don't understand.

Logically, your poor people are less healthy and more likely to be the primary incubators of pandemics, which can in turn threaten the rich. Terrorism breeds or finds support where education, economic, and sociopolitical opportunities are non-existent. The shortage of food and shelter, education, and jobs represents a loss of tax revenue, safety, quality of life, and an increase in security protection; all costs that impact the affluent. Visibly supporting justice and human rights would win loyalties of the impoverished that would indirectly but substantially reduce security costs alone. As I look at your numbers, the rich could get richer and more secure by proactively supporting enlightened, large-scale programs in health, education, welfare, and civil-rights for the poor. If anything, the financially and politically powerful seem to resist such initiatives. Don't they know what poverty retention costs them financially? This seems quite paradoxical to me.

Actually, this one I've puzzled over quite a bit myself. How do you see it?

It is multifaceted and my spreadsheet of the details is cluttered because it must differentiate the very from slightly affluent, the new from old money, the knowledgeable from unenlightened, the politically networked from isolated, the religious from secular.

Yes, we need that level of detail at least. Another thought is that in order to get richer than my neighbors I must have successfully competed against them, treating and perceiving them as opponents or enemies. It's hard to suddenly reverse and see them as my brothers who are deserving of my help, especially if that reorientation reminds me that I was not very philanthropic in moving up. Similarly, inheritors of wealth, if becoming generous to the poor, might have to perceive their benefactors as having been overly self-serving or even ruthless.

But isn't there a great deal of philanthropy here?

Yes, indeed, and far more so than in most other countries, but still a small percentage of private wealth accumulations. And most sums are not donated to poverty alleviation but rather to other worthy causes: the local ballet troupe, urban beautification program, religious organizations, medical research, or scholarships for the elite. Very little gets to programs in development or rehabilitation which directly alleviates poverty.

What other barriers does your spreadsheet highlight?

Many of the few well-intentioned poverty programs are ineffective because they address a single facet of poverty, such as health or housing, jobs or education, rather than adopting a holistic strategy. An enlightened education program is useless if no one in the immediate family has a job, and so forth.

Also, there is validity to the contention that graft, corruption, and mismanagement of well-meaning programs is pervasive. Often, the programs have no public accountability and the money supports the organization more than the people in need.

So potential donors see few examples of poverty programs having impact where intended. Of course, this is because almost by definition, the needy do not reside in supportive environments. Some portion of emergency supplies to earthquake victims will always migrate to the black market or an offshore bank account. This waste tends to keep philanthropy on its more prosaic pathways.

Fascinating! Yet your donors don't seem to mind that typically less than 2-5 percent of their costly medications and vitamins are absorbed, with the rest wasted.

Good point. Then there's the gratitude problem. Even when the relief process begins working productively, donors will be greeted with snarls of "What took you so long? It's not enough." If the programs are finally functioning successfully and are well-integrated into relief and development processes, the many voices claiming credit for that success will drown out any recognition of the original donors. This phenomenon often occurs whether the donor has adopted a child, contributed to a relief or development program, a community, or a region.

I'm afraid there's another factor, which is almost silly. Affluence acquired and retained in playing by the rules evokes distance, even antagonism, toward those who are less successful. The attitude develops that losers, rather than deserving help, deserve to be punished, since they have ignored the winner's self-discipline and gratification postponement. Either they didn't play by the rules, or they rejected the game and its rules, or didn't play hard enough to deserve help. Donating to the loser would be gifting the unwashed, undeserving, and yes, the potential iconoclast or anarchist—all of which violates the donor's Calvinistic, disciplined upbringing.

Somehow they'll have to stop feeling that they're contributing an undeserved gift and start seeing it as a membership fee.

Can you explain that?

Yes, but later. You seem to suggest that diagramming the stakeholders in sufficient detail will explain all paradoxes. Will that be the case for some of my other paradoxes in energy, pandemics, criminal justice, or education?

Well, wherever an unproductive situation persists that has available remedies, there is usually a stakeholder involved, maintaining the status quo. Often, this is done deliberately, but sometimes inadvertently, by applying the wrong remedy to a misdiagnosed situation; counter-terrorism is a good example. Sometimes the paradox persists, as in the case of rape, due to the absence of stakeholders with the power or understanding or mechanisms or will to make changes.

A final caution: We've explained several paradoxes by moving to a higher level of aggregation in the system. But remember, it's not always a matter of system aggregation level. Some paradoxes would disappear irrespective of stakeholder anomalies and shortcomings if technologies were substantially improved, such as a vaccine for AIDS or a plan for alternative energy—or if more patient investors could be mobilized for demonstrably high-profit science and education programs.

That's helpful. Now let me ask, having demystified a paradox in terms of stakeholder inconsistencies and advocated the appropriate remedies, what would be next?

Frequently, the stakeholder with power to apply the prescribed remedy doesn't choose to do so. Finding out why and what to do about it can be more challenging than the systems analysis that yielded the prescribed diagnosis. Does the stakeholder lack the right conceptual models or values or environment? Maybe it's the absence of motivation or information or technology. Even simple flowcharting at this level can clarify and provide useful insights about where next to look in detail. For example, if motivation is the dominant barrier to change, elements of motivation at the next level of detail can be charted, such as risk of the unknown or nostalgia for the known, joys of retribution, a disconnect in time, or institutions between the risk and reward takers.

You seem quite facile with our paradox-demystification process.

That's probably because it's a natural part of assessing the situation, which is often the first thing we do in science or technology. Once we understand what's happening, or think will happen, we decide whether we need to change something, including research, to help that understanding. You've told me that my planet is about to implode, and that's a situation I don't like. So I want to learn from you what "saved" planets look like in order to develop our own survival plan. Have you any wisdom to offer in this immediate context?

Wisdom? Probably not, but I could make the observation that too many of Earth's stakeholders with control of key resources and institutions have apparently been so focused on the acquisition and retention of their power that they are dangerously myopic and anachronistic. Just in long-term, parochial self-interest, they need to assimilate or somehow accommodate stakeholders with science, technology, information, and understanding of the key elements of long-term survival.

Same time tomorrow, OK?

Absolutely.

Session 19

Well ... you've convinced me that mapping the stakeholders and the periphery of systems can be helpful in understanding my paradoxes. But is that all?

No, there's much more. The power and broad applicability of systems analysis and design is hard to convey. I've often used a system as conceptual framework for helping me to understand everything from global issues to my interpersonal relationships and inner relationship with myself. But most people don't understand systems, let alone consider how useful systems thinking and tools can be in their own lives.

Frankly, it seems both impenetrable and boring at the same time.

Well, that's where you're wrong. The apparent impenetrability is a combination of the shorthand jargon we use and the fact that most of us systems people are not especially good communicators. Also, the more exciting and challenging applications involve lots of mathematics, and mathematics seems boring. Because it's usually presented devoid of its applications, mathematics seems incomprehensible, hence a turn-off and impossible to learn, like anything else that's a turn-off. But when you look at or work with systems, trust me; it's exciting and powerful stuff.

So tell me more about systems.

OK, here's the entire story in one paragraph. As I sketched for you at the outset, a system has one or more purposes, inputs, and outputs. Every system has its stakeholders. It exists in its environment, sometimes within another system or super system. Internally, every system is composed of a bunch of interacting parts or subsystems, each of which may be composed of other interconnected subsystems, the most detailed of which may be composed of components. That's it. And like anything else, a system has its life cycle that begins with requirements that determine performance specification, then design and development, construction and installation, utilization and maintenance, revision, maybe more such cycles, and ultimately retirement.

Gripping. You're sounding so generic, I'm afraid you've lost me again. Do you communicate with your family this way too?

Well, I'm divorced and my two children are away at college. But just from body language alone, I can assure you that Teresa and Sam are wide-eyed and totally attentive whenever I'm close by. I don't even have to say very much.

Yes, but aside from your goldfish ...

OK, maybe another systems example would help. Let's see ... here's one: when I teach a new course, I design it as a system.

I don't understand.

I write out the course's purpose, then its desired outputs. In particular, I want the students to understand certain concepts, acquire facility with certain tools or procedures, and learn where to go for more depth or breadth. Corresponding to this statement of outputs, I list the inputs, including the requirement that students enter with certain prerequisites, capabilities, and intentions and that sufficient laboratory facilities, libraries, and textbook choices are available. At that point, I can design the course structure and content, with the necessary test and control mechanisms. See? It's a systems approach.

Got it. And then?

Well, after teaching the course once, I examined the test and evaluation results—my own evaluations as well as student evaluations. I discovered that much of the course material didn't work well when presented as a lecture. Some of the students had learned what they wanted from the textbook, at least at a descriptive level. So they got nothing useful but an attendance check-off from coming to class. Other students hadn't learned from the textbook assignment, or hadn't even read it, so they couldn't quite follow the lecture. I had discovered a weak component in my system!

So what did you do?

Well, not to bore you with details, but some of the course contained controversial content, so I organized student teams to debate these issues, for which they needed to assimilate the background material before class. For other class sessions, I announced that there would be no lecture, but that I would only answer their prepared questions. In effect, I'd replaced weak system components with more effective ones.

Another example?

Let's See. I "persuaded" my son to examine his college application choices by means of a systems approach: identifying inputs, short-and long-term outputs, and decision criteria. He was initially reluctant to do this until reminded of where some of the system inputs would be coming from, i.e., tuition dollars.

His ultimate spreadsheet confronted him with the realization that his primary decision criterion of "student life"—more specifically, girls, beer, and sports, should be augmented with some academic and career criteria as well. This systems approach gave him some insights, and his father some peace of mind without damaging the friendship. This example reminds me to mention that sometimes merely engaging in the systems analysis process can be more valuable than specific results of the analysis.

Interesting. Another example?

There's much more to say about systems. But right now I'd be interested in hearing more of how you, as a resident from a planet that's made it, perceive us as we grapple with our technology shocks.

I'll try to oblige, but for context, it would help me to first understand more of how you conduct your science policies and how your S&T institutions are structured. Just a bit of the flavor would help our exchanges, I believe. Maybe tomorrow?

That's fine. Tomorrow, our regular time.

I'd also like to hear more about your mystery lady, especially if what you feel and think about her relates at all to issues and ideas we've been discussing.

I don't want to talk about her, but … my initial fantasy was just about sex and then shifted into a cerebral mode. I wanted to understand how she thinks and processes her cognitive issues. But then I found myself fantasizing that she and I would become friends. No, more than that. Rather, that we'd become companions, soul mates, contributors to each other's growth with shared, enriching experience in both intellectual and aesthetic dimensions. Right about now, I'm wishing that you and I were in e-mail rather than chat mode, I'd erase all this blabbering before sending it to you. It's not at all like me, or at least I don't think so. Does it say anything to you about the human condition on my planet?

Yes and no. I'd been trying to understand if your one-on-one relationships have relevance to your relationships between countries or cultures. I think I need more data.

Tomorrow?

By all means.

SESSION 20

Shall we continue?

Sure, but I don't want to talk about my mystery lady right now. It's embarrassing because I hardly know her, so my chatter yesterday may have been mostly about my private fantasies that I don't feel a need or desire to share with an extraterrestrial, no matter how receptive. Maybe after my next dinner with her I'll have some insight about relationships to share, but for now, let's move on. No offense.

So, in our early e-mail and chats, you seemed more than a little contemptuous of how we handle our science and technology. You implied that the planetary instability in our immediate future could be attributed at least in part to our mishandling of S&T. I'm curious as to how an allegedly more advanced civilization runs S&T, and also if you still feel as contemptuous about ours now that you are a bit more indoctrinated.

Let me apologize once again for my early attitude. Given the history and circumstances, I've come to believe that you do quite well, deserve applause for some—but it just isn't good enough. It borders on the ludicrous.

How so, my galaxy-guru? Incidentally, I'll bet that macho know-it-all attitude really attracts your ET lady friends up there. No wonder your playmates encouraged you to take this distant assignment.

Look, I don't deserve your sarcasm. I initially came to observe, not to help. So now I'm trying to help, without quite knowing why. I'm sorry to not be more upbeat, but as your playmates say here, "don't shoot the messenger." And for the record, my close friends are mostly male.

Oops, that hadn't occurred to me. OK, let's get on with it. This S&T policy topic may be vital to implementing whatever roadmap we develop. I need to know what you think we're doing wrong and what your more advanced society does right.

I agree that this topic is vital. I wish your brethren behaved as if they agreed. Here are my notes I'll email to you.
NOTES:

- *As elsewhere, Earth's S&T enhances large-scale economic, military, and political power. But mindlessly applied, it can have either very positive or very adverse consequences. Natural resources are depleted as toxic effluents increase.*

- *Automation-displaced jobs cause global unemployment. Work is no longer a viable income redistribution mechanism, an education motivator, or a sociopolitical pacifier. This in turn weakens the middle class' role as the rich-poor linkage.*

- *Communication technologies in the hands of political and religious leaders promote sanctity of "their" life, a value deeply instilled by evolution in any successful species.*

- *Wars are won or lost based on technological advantage.*

All of which suggests a less-than-cavalier attitude toward S&T pol-icy would be appropriate. Nothing is properly synchronized or even sequenced in order. Progress in information science seems far ahead of S&T in materials and energy. These in turn are more advanced than in life sciences—although molecular biology and brain research seem to be getting attention, now that they've finally devised instrumentation more powerful than a magnifying glass. But they don't recognize synergies between humanities and science. What's more confusing is that 150 years ago, it was just the oppo-site, with the humanities and the arts leading science.

Of further confusion to me is the variety of <u>roles</u> *played by S&T: sometimes as an effective detonator for change, other times as a pas-sive enabler, and sometimes even a roadblock. There's no pattern.*

Examining the <u>sources</u> *of S&T doesn't help clarify matters. Much of the basic science seems to have been pure serendipity, often from some socially maladjusted scientists with plenty of time for research in the absence of other diversions. Their basic science has, of course, proven extremely valuable relative to the meager resources it requires. Earthlings have benefited enormously from science in wartime, presiding over breakthroughs in nuclear physics, surveil-lance, communication, and aerospace.*

From which I'd expected to find a long-standing policy of at least nurturing scarce research talent while throwing money at emerging threats and opportunities—just as we do at home. Wrong. Every-thing seems extemporaneous. Does America suddenly need scientists to help fight a war? No problem: the world's best and brightest come right over as refugees. Then, immediately after the war, everybody forgets about science and just dashes around making money by applying the government-funded S&T to civilian products. In peacetime, they allocate a mere one-half of one percent of Gross National Product to science, and most of that is probably for applied rather than basic science. If they merely reapplied 1/10ᵗʰ of one percent of the profits derived from previous research to subsequent research budgets—it seems so obvious.

Digging deeper, I find that there's almost always an inherent mismatch between their requirements for S&T progress and the organizational goals of their home institutions. Investment in pure science seldom repays the investors quickly enough. Scientists insist on sharing information with their peers and basic science intrinsically can't be protected as intellectual property. Even within private industry, their corporate research centers exist precariously unless they directly support an important product line of the firm. Most universities do some research, but primarily as a means for enhancing visibility and facilities, or to attract faculty and students; the actual research results are of secondary concern. Government laboratories are constrained by bureaucracy or a narrow mandate. Of the few basic research entities around, much of their work seems directed at keeping the monster test facility occupied and the funds flowing, irrespective of how the research priorities fit actual needs and opportunities.

So I reluctantly conclude that maybe I have been looking for something too sophisticated. Maybe investors and companies just do what has worked before because it has worked before. They wait until an application needs some basic science, then throw money at it and hire the best refugees around.

That said, now I wonder if what has worked so well before will continue to work as well in the future. Of course, letting applications dictate research agendas assures results relevant to markets, efficient utilization of resources, and of scientists. But basic research often has generic, unpredictable value. Even Earthlings should be able to see that the science underlying genetically modified crops per-

tains to pharmaceuticals or ecology as well. Basic research costs so little relative to ultimate benefits. END OF NOTES

Good observations, but things aren't as bleak as you portray. For example, one encouraging trend in all this is an increasing involvement of our private sector in pure science. Private investors, especially venture capitalists, entrepreneurs, and company executives these days are discovering science's value as precursor to proprietary technologies. Now some of those knowledgeable about and affluent from their own technologies; they are starting to recognizing that pure science spawns, and provides an edge in, technology exploitation. So these investors are investing, lobbying government, donating to universities, establishing foundations—all targeted at multiple fields of science. Much of it is profit-driven, oriented to establishing a patent base, attracting talent, creating markets, and making money. Fortunately, we seem able to also derive important sociopolitical and institutional benefits from such financially oriented activities. I don't quite get how that works, but it seems to, at least here in America.

That is encouraging. Nevertheless, I find it surprising and regrettable that there is so little centralized, pure science policy, priorities, and programs. It's sort of a shame. America's man-to-the-moon race, actually quite complex and challenging, demonstrated what you can do with a prioritized, committed, focused program. In thinking about it, just a few such programs could solve lots of important problems, maybe even help effectuate the planet's survival.

With all due respect to your more advanced civilization, I think you are being too harsh, perhaps even superficial, in your assessments. Our more creative practitioners and managers somehow get the job done. That's even though the knowledgeable people who work and think and write about S&T seem to have little influence over it. And decisions are made by politicians whose personal exposure to science appears to have been limited to cosmetic surgery and teeth whitening.

That sounds right. And here is the concluding piece of my notes.

NOTES: I've tried to understand the disparity in maturity of Earth's technologies; some are almost quaint while others are highly advanced. In particular, Earthlings do not aggressively promote science that could foster technologies vital to developing:

- *Fast maritime cargo ship;*

- *Tools facilitating exploration and extraction of ocean floor resources;*

- *Counters to terrorism, cyber-crime, counterfeiting, tax evasion, and money laundering;*

- *Non-lethal weapons;*

- *Responsive infrastructures for pandemics and large-scale addictions;*

- *Contraception and conception aids;*

- *Self-managed health, education, and psychological development of individuals, relationships, families, and communities; and*

- *Safe nuclear energy generation, control, and waste treatment.*

On the other hand, to their credit, coming soon are systems for substantially improved:

- *Wind and wave energy;*

- *Energy conversion, transmission, and storage;*

- *Water desalinization;*

- *Tools, tests, and remedies for medical clinical practice;*

- *Computer aids to education; and*

- *Information acquisition and dissemination.*

And of course, most highly developed already are:

- *Toys for children and adults;*

- *Recreation and spectator sports systems;*

- *Food and drug products for upscale markets;*

- *Mass advertising and promotion systems; and*

- *Military systems and equipments.*

END OF NOTES

I'm impressed! You've really been working. Why don't you quit your musicology game and join my consulting practice? OK, not a good idea ... my clients already think they've got an ET consultant. So in summary?

In summary, you do rather well in S&T development and application, except perhaps in human development; both behavioral and social sciences. Most surprising are the meager programs, budgets, and institutions devoted to pure science. Your institutions that conduct pure research are almost all dedicated to other missions with science peripheral. Just because its high benefit/cost won't directly benefit initial investors is no reason to continue short-changing pure science. Bad planning and prioritizing of S&T got you into this mess; let sensible policies and programs help get you out.

Do you do such a fine job on your planet?

It's hard to discuss in detail, here and out of context. But in a quick summary, we have great respect, almost reverence, and unlimited resources for pure science, with open disclosure and availability to all comers. On the other hand, we are very careful about how its application or technologies are authorized and disseminated. Those opportunities are preceded by exhaustive assessment of potential impacts—more sociopolitical than economic, and the consequences, both adverse and favorable, with ongoing monitoring and auditing of implementation. We have developed and constantly refine similar policies and institutions in utilizing energy, materials and information; all crucial to sustaining an advanced civilization.

Admittedly we have traditionally exploited S&T almost mindlessly. Your planet's experience suggests that proactive fostering of smart S&T policies can greatly leverage what we need here and now. That's a powerful message I want to think about carefully. Tomorrow, our regular time?

I wouldn't miss it!

SESSION 21

Sorry I've been out of touch for a few days. Work piled up and I've been more than a little preoccupied. Let's see, where did we leave off? Oh yes. I'd written myself a note to ask you to summarize where you think we are. I would like to know how you, as an objective, experienced outsider, see my planet's situation and what we might do about it all.

I'm relieved to hear from you. I was concerned that you or your computer might be indisposed. I'm a bit preoccupied myself at the moment, but from my recent interviews, eavesdropping, and Internet searches, I have some observations on ... I wonder if I've described you Earthlings adequately, especially the degree to which you retain your evolutionary legacies while grappling—somewhat nobly, I would add, with ever accelerating socioeconomic and political challenges.

You're probably doing a fine job. It's just that my brain is elsewhere at the moment.

Me too. What's your excuse?

I don't really want to discuss it. Well, OK ... the dinner date with my mystery lady last Monday night went considerably beyond dinner, extending into breakfast and we've been together constantly, seamlessly, passionately ever since. I've always dealt with new situations by analysis, dealing with the component parts one by one. Looking into her eyes drives out all that analytically explicit stuff. Whatever cognitive processes may be intact are subliminal … listen to this drivel, I no longer know how to form coherent thoughts and don't seem to mind.

Me too.

You too? Why do you keep saying "me too?"

Haven't you guessed? I'm her—your mystery woman.

OK, I guess I knew you'd make a joke out of it. That's why I didn't want to bring it up in the first place.

No, I'm her. Really. You automatically assumed that I was male. It didn't even occur to you to ask! Had you asked, here's proof: I wore a red dress at Monday's dinner, then very little for the next three days, a polka-dot skirt this morning after a breakfast of coffee with pancakes, slightly overcooked due to intervening priorities. We agreed to reconvene tomorrow night … will we?

I don't know. I don't know what to say. I don't know who or what you are. Who am I?

I'm just as disoriented, even though I've had more time to think about things. It's probably better if we don't meet tomorrow. Why don't we continue the e-mail and chat-room for a while as if nothing had happened? Then we'll see. Is that all right with you?

Yes, I think so … OK … whatever you say. Tomorrow, regular time.

Session 22

So where are we? What about us?

There is no "us" right now. We agreed to focus on work for ... and I have very little time left.

That's not fair. First you told me you had to go back to your planet, and then you said that you'd delay. You know that I don't want you to leave. Talk to me, please.

I don't want to leave. Our work is important—you are important to me. I've never felt like this. My lifetime friends at home recognize that I'm not the same and are quite worried. In fact, they are waiting for my signal to come rescue me from the cult or kidnappers they suspect are holding me. If I told them that I'm being held by a systems engineer whose other suit is at the cleaners, probably from his last oil change ... I'm sorry. I don't know whether to laugh or cry, and seem to be doing a lot of both these days. Maybe they should come rescue me. I need to sort it all out for myself. Now can we please get back to work?

Yes, good idea. I need to stay focused. I'm beginning to appreciate your heritage of integrity and communication without lies or nuances. In that same vein, I must tell you that I feel the same. You express my feelings exactly. I even have a friend or two who would try to rescue me, or at least send a shrink, if I confided being held in thrall by an extraterrestrial. ☺

OK, so let's proceed with our work. Where did we leave off?

In summary, once again: economies of scale plus the demographics have produced high-density, high-growth populations. These had historically been tightly controlled by tribalism's membership benefits with associated behavioral rewards and punishments. Now suddenly, information, weapons, mobility, and greater affluence are widely available. Uncontrolled proliferation of WMD and mass communication erode the traditional mechanisms for maintenance of preferential power structures such as governments, industries, military, and religions. That's the basic. Drug abuse, AIDS, energy, environment, and cultural difference—these factors only accentuate the challenge, but challenge it is.

Is it hopeless?

I thought so initially, but maybe not. You humans seem to have a unique resiliency and adaptability. Also, you have the necessary resources, knowledge, and expertise to fix things as we have on our planet. So I'm hopeful in principle. But your leaders, institutions, and organizations are woefully antiquated in confronting these new challenges. Too often, the knowledge and expertise needed resides in people without access to leadership positions or control of the resources or institutions that require reconfiguring. The resource owners became such by being especially talented and motivated as hunter-gather-warrior's. Still into rape, pillaging, and superstition, they've been successful for so long that they've felt no need or interest in dealing with the rest of the planet's population. In essence, past success has made you very vulnerable to the future.

So how do we move on? What would we need to change?

There might be many answers to your question. But if my planet is the model, ultimately you'll need to change the perceptions and convictions of Earthlings, including your modes of leadership selection, information access, and processing. The people with wealth and power have achieved and maintained power by dedicated, focused self-interest. In the future, out of self-interest, they must become more "socialistic or very dedicated philanthropists, to preserve their power. In a sense, to remain the elite class they must now learn that acquiring future wealth—and survival, lies in nurturing their society holistically.

Over time, a major cultural change must occur. The affluent must understand that it is to their own benefit to help other tribes who have done nothing for them and will probably not even reciprocate or express gratitude. At the same time, the powerless must come to believe that food, potable water, shelter, justice, and upward mobility can be acquired more advantageously by collaboration with the "establishment" rather than by destroying it. And enlightened modes of leadership selection become a necessary, but not sufficient, condition for all factions.

Modes of leadership selection? What's wrong with how we do it here? Isn't it much better here than almost anywhere else?

Yes, but no longer good enough. The problems increasingly call for leadership expertise rather than charm and connectedness. The universal franchise for voters works only to the extent that voters are sufficiently educated and informed to vote wisely, and that the votes get counted properly. You could fix your voter fraud problem quickly with technology and a bit of political will, but there isn't time to educate and maintain currency of knowledge and involvement among all citizens—maybe sometime in the distant future. In the very short term, you could do what we did, which was to co-opt the mass media networks, then certify and market the qualified candidates. We were very successful in this by establishing a high-visibility, respected council for rating the candidates on competence and values. Also, rather than artificial TV debates, we put each candidate into unrehearsed decision-making "game" situations which would be telecast—very revealing and edifying for voters.

Aren't you needlessly pessimistic? We've been through technology driven "revolutions" before: agriculture, military, industry, and now the information revolution. The next technology revolution has always rescued us throughout history. We are adaptable and opportunistic, and our institutions are much more durable, flexible, and organized than you seem to think. Check it out.

I've been doing just that and here are my notes. Check your email.

NOTES: Their "information revolution" does appear to be different in its unprecedented pace and breadth. It seems to increase aggregate wealth by productivity increases. Unlike previous revolutions, this increase appears to be faster and broader with less potential risk, postponing the backlash that usually follows revolution. In this instance, that backlash is muted, or keeps getting postponed, as new technologies, products, and markets continue to proliferate.

Information technologists and entrepreneurs have benefited enormously. More functionality is constantly being inserted into standardized hardware and software building blocks, displacing computer-related jobs at the component and system language level precipitously. But the transition is relatively painless because of rapidly expanding product alternatives and applications that drive new market demand, creating jobs designing customized systems assembled from new building blocks.

This process replicates as building block assemblages become standardized, displacing the designers but not before the need expands for more people at the applications and systems levels. Arithmetic, algebra, and trigonometry used to be popular subjects to study, serving as the basis for careers as surveyors, accountants, navigators, and structural designers. Now those subjects are all available on a silicon chip. Business administration is currently a popular degree and career, but its content is increasingly available in software. So what's next?

Products and markets traditionally reliant on consumer ignorance including substantial elements of insurance, advertising, health care, and financial services are becoming disrupted as more factual information becomes accessible to buyers. Similarly, enterprises that only compile and transfer increasingly available information without adding value, like brokerages, libraries, and sales agencies are similarly endangered long-term. Value added, hence new products and services associated with information systems, will increasingly tend to concentrate at the system interfaces between the sources and/or end-users.

For example, the radio-directed policeman who apprehends the suspect may not know whether she was guided by DNA or fingerprint matching, by satellite surveillance, or profile databases. The primary added value shifts from the field to police headquarters where intelligent selection of many sensing modalities and management of the data systems will predominate in importance.

As another example, value added in facilities' site selection will reside increasingly in choosing the pertinent type of information from an enormous collection of data bases: remote sensing, fine-grain demographics, cell phone or vehicular traffic, and more. Knowing what questions to ask and then making the proper interpretations for decision-making will be increasingly more vital than merely acquiring and massaging databases. At home, the importance of asking the right questions and interpreting the answers for enlightened decision-making is self-evident. I'm appalled at how Earthlings design and conduct, then misconstrue and misapply simple attitude surveys for market research or public relations work, even when no deceptive result is intended.

Durable enterprises will always add value that customers can't easily generate for themselves. The information revolution undoubtedly will continue to expand opportunities for a diversity of new products and services. Requisite specialists and their employers will do well in this volatile environment. But watch out! Your continuing economic growth and prosperity derive largely from market demand for discretionary or luxury products and services; affordable because technology facilitates hiring low-paid, unskilled labor. But with the increasing number of unskilled workers who can't afford luxuries, where will future market growth come from? END OF NOTES

These particular comments of yours, erudite and cogent as always ... they convey some kind of subliminal feeling. I'm not sure, but it's as if you are preoccupied, perhaps with a different sort of question. Might that be the one I posed before: what about us?

Yes, indeed. I had no idea that Earthlings could pick up—it must be our emotional proximity. Well, that actually helps me decide to tell you what I need to. Tomorrow, same time, OK?

Absolutely.

Session 23

Our last chat on systems left me wondering about a few things. In particular, from your flexible attitude about system definitions, there must be an exceedingly wide variety of systems. And every system must be different and forbiddingly complex.

I'm wondering if you really care about system complexity. Or is this just a filler to postpone addressing our relationship's complexity?

No. I'm genuinely interested and concerned about both. But if you don't mind, I'd like us to deal with our relationship at the end rather than the beginning of this session.

OK. You just asked about how we deal with complexity. That question, like several others you've posed, can be answered descriptively as if you're a tourist—which, in a sense, is what you are. Answering you in that way doesn't empower you to use the powerful tools for dealing with complexity. It might reassure you or excite you enough to read a book or take a course in order to use the tools. But in any case, the concepts, perspectives, and even some techniques of the system tools can often be very helpful in messy decision situations, so there's value at even this "descriptive" level we've been playing with.

OK. My expectations are hereby adjusted. And let me confide that I have actually been reading some systems books "offline." I started doing so initially because what you were saying ... well I suspected you might be a bit "unbalanced" or maybe even a comic. But then I gradually concluded that either you were sane or my books' authors were fruitcakes too.

Reading books? That explains why your questions go beyond what I'd expect from a musicologist much of the time. Incidentally, I confess that consorting with my musicologist friend has left me more than a bit "unbalanced." So if I wasn't initially, I certainly am now. ☺

OK. So we partially control complexity by ignoring extraneous elements of the system. It sounds arbitrary; I suppose. In configuring the system, we'll exclude those inputs, outputs, and overly detailed subsystems if they are irrelevant to system behavior and/or our purpose. You might recall that in describing our office heating system we didn't bother to mention the safety regulator in the heater that would prevent overheating. We also didn't explicitly include extraneous heat sources, such as sunshine and warm air from outside, or machinery and office occupants. These would be included if our purpose was different, for example to determine the required heater capacity.

Even as an ET I can see how ignoring irrelevant inputs and outputs must help to keep things simple. But let's don't keep this conversation overly simple too. Are you seeing me as your t-shirt lady?

Absolutely not!

OK, sorry for the interruption. Please proceed.

Right. Where was I? Yes, OK. In addition to care in deciding what needs to be explicit rather than implicit, also we can often organize lots of details by means of generic commonalities. For instance, although each stakeholder's primary role may be distinctive—the system's architect, entrepreneur, investor, or designer, we can utilize generic descriptors applicable to every stakeholder: culture, resources, and capabilities. Thus, you might profile each stakeholder's attributes in a table such as the one I'm sending you as an e-mail attachment. Tabular entries might also be drawn from a small generic set designed for the specific purpose.

Yes, I can see how at minimum, that's a way to focus rational debate to the relevant issues of concern.

STAKEHOLDER PROFILES

STAKEHOLDER ROLES → STAKEHOLDER ATTRIBUTES ↓	Architect	Entrepreneur	Designer	Builder	Manager
Culture, values and beliefs					
Strengths and weaknesses					
Education, knowledge and information					
Goals and capabilities					
Intentions and plans					

Exactly. For example, suppose an incomprehensible anomaly is occurring. The diagram may help determine if the cause is a dis-

connect between those stakeholders with power versus stakeholders with information. Alternatively, it may be inadequate
cognition capabilities, mismatched goals and means, or whatever. Paradoxes are resolved, and cul-de-sacs illuminated, checklists for detailed data gaps, and the like—and all of it without
necessarily resorting to complex mathematical models.

*Do you have any other ways to simplify how you conceptualize
systems and what you do with them?*

Sure. We just talked about using generic descriptors to work
with stakeholders' attributes, which is helpful because there are
so many attributes of so many diverse systems. Similarly, since
there may be a multitude of inputs and outputs for one or several different systems we can resort to their generic descriptors.

*I'm sure if I'd been born and raised, here I'd be able to under-
stand what you just said.* ☺

OK, look. A system's principle input or output might be
almost anything: cookie dough, electricity, weather reports—all
radically different, right? But each of these is a member of its
general category: cookie dough is a material, electricity is
energy, and weather reports are information. The system itself
can be characterized as a structure or processor of its inputs. The
elements of our producer economy, what we produce, buy, and
sell; they all fit within one of these general categories.

*But aren't the "categories" each a necessary attribute of every
commodity? For any one of these attributes to manifest, you need
them all, at least in the physical world. A book, for example, is a
commodity that contains information, which is why you buy it. But
without its ink and paper (materials), at a temperature, thermal
(energy), that wouldn't burn or freeze your hands, you wouldn't
buy it.*

You're right. Not bad for a musicologist! So it's actually more useful to put it in terms of the commodity's attribute of interest; that is, I'm buying the book for its information, not for its ink and paper.

OK. So that's a very concise way to catalog system inputs and outputs. Can you be as concise in describing the system itself?

I think so. Broadly speaking, the system OUTPUTS result from processing its INPUTS. The PROCESS consists of merging or separating, converting, or transferring the INPUTS.

Can you mention examples of how your systems can be cataloged according to these three descriptors?

I thought you'd never ask.☺ In the rudimentary table I'm sending to you by e-mail, the coal power plant is located where it is because it CONVERTS its coal INPUT into its power OUTPUT. Here's another example: A TV newscast program is a system whose INPUTS are INFORMATION. These inputs are then CONVERTED as OUTPUT INFORMATION to hopefully discerning audiences.

That's impressive. Any system in your world can be classified this simply! Incidentally why "hopefully discerning?"

Oh, that's just my reminder of the newscast system's several uninvited inputs which if ignored, pervert the system output. Every system has them and a good system design will anticipate and safeguard the system accordingly. Your newscast system has reporters whose sources are incomplete or contaminated with extraneous inputs and system owners who will inject inputs to please their attorneys, audiences, and advertisers.

Interesting. So if you wanted to improve the quality of newscast programs, you might first sketch the system, its various desired and undesired inputs, and maybe segment audiences by their characteristics. Then from this sketch, you'd devise a spreadsheet from which problems and potential solutions could be identified and prioritized in detail.

I didn't mean to get into all that, but yes. Mainly, I thought you'd be interested to see that we can classify any and all systems in a simple table whose rows and columns are system inputs and outputs. A further dimension or generic descriptor is the system process, i.e., merge, separate, convert, or transfer for producing its outputs from inputs. This is another example of how systems people organize and grapple with systems complexity.

INPUTS → OUTPUTS ↓ *PROCESS*	Materials	Energy	Information
Materials *Merge* *Separate* *Convert* *Transfer*			
Energy *Merge* *Separate* *Convert* *Transfer*	Coal Power Plant	Electrical grid	
Information *Merge* *Separate* *Convert* *Transfer*		Thermometer	News broadcast system Communication satellite

This looks like a powerful classification framework. Does it always work?

It is quite general as you can see. The idea of tabulating things in terms of their generic categories always works. The particular choices of rows and columns may vary. For example this particular chart might not be the one I'd chose for tabulating human services systems.

What if I need to work with the system's internal subsystems at a more detailed level?

The system can be represented as a grouping of subsystems and/or subsystems of subsystems depicted as boxes interconnected by linkages depicted as arrows with occasional junctions. The arrows just <u>transfer</u> the commodities. The junctions <u>merge/separate</u> commodities while each box <u>converts</u> its incoming commodities into its local outputs. Internal to the processor you'd find more arrows, junctions and boxes, just more transfer and convert, merge and separate. So if you needed to describe the system configuration in words (frightening thought) you'd just need a few verbs: transfer (arrows), convert (boxes) and combine or separate (junctions) for virtually any kind of system.

This sounds very useful.

Yes, it's another generic simplifier. In order to produce products and services you simply must first <u>collect the raw inputs</u>, then process them. The inputs are simply combinations of <u>material, energy, and information</u>. Similarly required for all this activity are the external <u>infrastructures and structures</u> and for developing and implementing the controlling <u>policies, plans and specifications</u> for finding, processing, and using the end <u>products and services</u>. So yes, there's a very wide diversity of stuff, but it's all compiled from this very small number of generic commodities and processes sketched below. The complexity resides in the aggregated configurations, not in the individual basic building blocks.

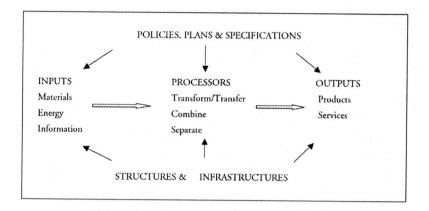

So what I get out of all this is that the analyst or designer can conceptualize and delineate anything as a system which can be ascribed a primary purpose and is composed of subsystems and subsystems of subsystems ad infinitum. Its generic building blocks are mercifully few in kind because they are generic and because the system's internal subsystems and external context or environment can be depicted by means of the same generic building blocks. Have I got that right?

Yes. Of course, this just pertains to the system structural configuration which is often all that you need sometimes to resolve your paradoxes or begin to conceptualize new possibilities in an orderly manner.

What else might I "need?"

Ignoring your sardonic punctuation, at the system, subsystem, or externalities level you might need to know or analyze or design the process. The process determines how the outputs result from the inputs. It's the meat in the hamburger. It can be a qualitative description or a quantitative mathematical model, that is, something quantitative. And you can work at a very wide range of mathematical sophistication; whatever fits the need. All of which means you can apply systems tools to any "system" and work at whatever level of detail and mathematical sophistication you need.

That is powerful. Anything else?

I don't think so, except to note that your purpose, not the system's, could be any of several. You might just want to think about what's going on or some possibilities or hypotheses, sort of organized speculation. Or your purpose might be to better understand the situation, the problems and solution opportunities, the paradoxes, and the potential threats and opportunities. It can stay largely intuitive but organized, or get very analytic and quantitative, or some combination of these. You might be trying to predict how the system will or might behave under various scenarios. You might be designing, upgrading, evaluating, monitoring, or controlling an existing or new system, grappling with requirements of its resources versus performance versus risk. The same ideas, skills, concepts, and tools pertain regardless of your needs and their variety.

A concluding thought is that anything with a broad range of application, such as systems like the air you breathe, tends to become invisible, unappreciated, and difficult to understand. Some of the system ideas and tools, however, are simple, and worth appreciating, understanding, and applying.

That's helpful. And I didn't mean to be insulting with the quotation marks. Now as to our meeting again, I've given it considerable thought, as I'm sure you have. Briefly, I'm in favor of doing so if you agree.

I do.

Wait. It's conditional on our not getting physical again. That was delightful and very useful in furthering my understanding of how relationships work here—and totally disconcerting! But no further purpose would be served in our work by continuing the physical relationship and it might begin to affect our perceptions and judgments in further collaboration.

I totally agree. I've had the same thoughts and additionally, any serious emotional involvement would be complicated and/or painful when you go back home. Neither of us needs that. So how about dinner at our now favorite restaurant tomorrow night?

If you don't mind, I'd like to delay until next week. I need more time to mull things over. In the meantime, perhaps you could help me to better understand how you professional "S&T" people think and function. I'd like to walk around a bit, e-mail you my notes, and then discuss same over dinner. Does that work for you?

Sure. Same time tomorrow?

That's fine.

SESSION 24

As promised, here are my notes from observing and meeting with some of your S&T colleagues. Rather than waiting until our dinner meeting, feel free to comment as you get this attachment.

Sure. I'm ready.

NOTES: In ruminating about some of my interviews with S&T people, it struck me that some of the weirdness that goes on here must derive from the professionals themselves—how they practice individually and in groups. Although each profession has its distinctive character, one rather consistent pattern is their myopia and parochialism—almost a siege-like posture of each profession.

I'm beginning to understand where that might come from. Most professional investors in S&T don't seem to care or know much about S&T. They tend to be focused on being in the right marketplace and/or backing the right entrepreneurial management. Some will even boast about their ignorance of the technical "details," relegating S&T to the same category as labor or facilities; "just one of the unavoidable enablers that deplete profits". They might hire a "technical nerd" or two for cosmetics or for jargon translation, but that's about all.

The professional scientists seem primarily interested in their science. Some are altruists, seeking higher truths to benefit humanity. Many don't seem to work well with people. Almost none of them work in institutions which genuinely appreciation the scientist or his/her product. Supervisors' concerns are with institutional reputation, donor or sponsor satisfaction and visible relevance of the research to an application.

The most gifted engineers, technicians and applied scientists seem to be drawn into management, sales, or fundraising. Plans, programs, and budget allocations are usually determined by experts in management, finance, entrepreneurship, or accounting rather than in S&T.

Also, large, complex, and long-term programs suffer from a balkanization of all professions. System architects may have skillfully developed a balanced set of cost-effective program plans and specifications. But balance is not always the top priority when the architectural fee is a fixed percentage of total program cost. Designers may intervene with improvements or ways to correct the architects' "mistakes." Meanwhile, the client or end-user or system requirements may have changed. The lawyers, accountants, and contract specialists next intervene, with an eye on the customer, subcontractors, labor unions, and regulatory constraints; they also can change over time as does their institutional reach. Each seeks to be heard over the cries of "It can't be done" that emanate from manufacturing, quality control, field engineering, and the hapless end-users.

Complicating this diffusion of perspectives, orientation and responsibilities is the use of outside professional service firms, whose independence assures freedom from turf wars and company politics, yet each injects a new subculture and constraints. The CPA and law firms operate under relatively stringent canons here, in contrast to architectural and engineering firms, or health care and consult-

ing organizations. The services each profession provides derive from science, agreed-upon precedence, and/or predetermined standards set by the respective professional societies. Litigation avoidance and productivity challenges increasingly dominate creativity and customized treatment for client welfare. Accountants utilize approved but unrealistic depreciation schedules; profit and loss allocations over time and operational components are based on simplistic models of the organization. Physicians provide health care that minimizes malpractice risks and maximizes conformity to agency-approved treatment protocols rather than what is deemed optimal for the patient.

Apparently, over time, the professions and most of their practitioners became institutionalized; hospitals hired the clinicians, and pharmaceutical companies hired the biochemists and research physicians. Manufacturing firms hired the professional engineers and lawyers. Although some practitioners and professionals remained independent, and a few become gurus, professors, or advisors, they all become institutionalized to an extent and their professionalism deferred to the organizational culture and constraints of employers or customers.

When institutionalization is the way that valuable profession-based services are delivered, their costs can become exorbitant. Quality of services may suffer and the services may no longer be optimized for individual needs. Also diluted is the professional's responsibility for and influence over client welfare, and in safeguarding the professional's canons and livelihood. On the other hand, more clients can be served, and the overall variety and value of the services may improve substantially, even though no longer customized.

Within the professional organization, the uncertain, risky future imparts great power to incumbency. Existing programs and per-

sonal relationships, familiarity with a product, technology, process, or logo all work against change. This creates the impression of a change-resistant bureaucracy, organizational complacency, and/or conflicts of interest. Sometimes this impression is valid and sometimes justified, but not always.

Examining the actual delivery of "professional services," I could see lots of different hoof prints; evidence of lawyers, accountants, managers, politicians, architects, all having trampled over each others' trail. No wonder so little relevant, known, properly applied S&T can leak through. But actually, an intriguing attribute of Earthlings I find quite appealing is that they seem to care about everything, even when they appear not to. Anyone from our highly organized, analytic, stable, and tranquil civilization must be jolted on entering this adrenalin-saturated place. But I find myself beginning to enjoy it. These primitives are <u>alive,</u> still looking over their shoulder for menacing dinosaurs but starting new companies or new relationships simply because "it's Monday." END OF NOTES

Excellent comments. I think you're really starting to understand this place. Same time tomorrow?

Thank you. Yes, fine with me.

SESSION 25

I'm looking forward to our dinner meeting tomorrow night. Meanwhile is there anything else?

Yes. I have several questions from our last discussion of systems.

Such as?

Well, to start, your neat little taxonomy suggests that all systems are similar. Do they all behave pretty much the same way?

That would simplify life, but they don't. Some systems are designed to block or self-regulate against input disturbances, such as the office temperature control system or the automobile's cruise control system, which maintains constant speed regardless of hill/valley road variations. For some applications the system's output directly tracks the input commands, such as the automobile's power steering system responding to the driver's input commands, that is, the steering wheel position.

Are all your systems designed to do something specific in response to their inputs?

Yes, but the system design can't always achieve the stakeholder's purpose. Some systems exhibit exponential growth or exponential decline irrespective of the nominal inputs. The village population may grow or decline, responding to a shift in migration, birth, or mortality rates irrespective of the village chief's intent. The financial manager can't always achieve the percentage annual profit goal for the investment portfolio.

Are there other kinds of system behavior variations?

Yes, several. Some systems are inherently unstable, going off in response to the slightest stimulus of any kind. To complicate the picture further, the system itself, whether stable or unstable, may contain stable or unstable subsystems.

I don't understand.

For example, the sailboat is intrinsically stable. If you let go of the helm, tiller, sail, or whatever, a boat in a harbor or very calm sea will automatically head into the wind. In contrast, letting go of the speeding car's steering wheel will cause the vehicle to veer off the road exponentially. It's an intrinsically unstable system—as would be the diagnosis of the driver by any surviving passenger. It's also the same thing if steering a car or managing a company.

Managing a company?

Sure. In some sense, company management can be easier than steering a car because there is more time for correcting mistakes, and more people to blame for them. However, managing a company is usually more challenging because the company's roadmap and, indeed, what the result of management's steering moves will yield. These are all uncertain.

Suppose we have an inexperienced manager who, in hopes of impressing everyone, decides to follow an aggressive plan for growth. So he increases sales sharply by lowering prices and by shifting people from production to marketing. As the backlog builds and production falls behind, he switches everyone possible into production. The extra overtime pay, the lost production efficiency, and price reductions impact profit requiring price increases and personnel layoffs. In addition, the extended delivery delays and reduced sales force cause a sharp drop in sales, causing him to pull everyone back into marketing and the oscillatory pattern persists. Once the manager learns to anticipate and steer more smoothly, sales may increase, even exponentially, at some nominal percentage rate. It's a lot like learning to ride a bicycle, except the bicycle is less forgiving of mistakes and the blame can't be shared.

Villages, companies, cars; you make it sound like everything behaves exponentially.

Lots of systems we design or that occur in nature behave exponentially. Tumors, village populations, and fixed-interest investments grow exponentially until they don't. The tumor's blood supply eventually becomes restricted, the village acquires a wave of refugees, the bank crashes. But until such events occur, the mathematical model of an exponential works well.

You have discussed creating a model of the system more than once. It sounds important?

We build models for a variety of reasons. We may use a plastic scale model of a hospital to see how the internal lighting or traffic flow will turn out. We might assemble a focus group as a model of all voters, shoppers, or jurors, then test the outcome of contemplated initiatives. We can seldom afford to model all system aspects; just the ones necessary for the intended purposes. A miniature aircraft wing may be used as a model for testing aerodynamics in a wind tunnel rather than a full-scale replica of the entire airplane.

Do you ever model the past or are your models always predictive of the future?

Good question. We build lots of models of the past, such as archeological skeletons, or exhibits in museums depicting history. But if it's too cumbersome, expensive, or dangerous to use plastic or people, we often build the model out of mathematical relationships. Accountants do that all the time. Past performance recorded as the financial statement derives from a math model. The projected performance derives from a mathematical model for the future.

Do their models incorporate diagrams of stakeholders or system subsystems?

Not explicitly. The stakeholders who hire the accountants and run the company are listed separately and the others referenced by category only. The system diagram would be just one junction with lots of input and output arrows, so it's unnecessary. Where there are shared incomes or expenses among subsystems, the accountant uses a simple prorating formula. So the sort of structure diagrams we've been talking about wouldn't be especially useful.

What about the mathematical models you mentioned?

Mathematical relationships in accounting reports are just simple arithmetic, so an actual diagram is unnecessary. Calculating depreciation, benefits liability, asset valuations, *these* "mathematical models" can be much more complicated, certainly as to the underlying assumptions if not the actual mathematics. So they are relegated to fine-print footnotes, probably so they'll be ignored. Managing the enterprise requires more sophisticated conceptual models, which are increasingly augmented by quantitative, mathematical models—many of which the accountants understand. Sophisticated models are occasionally employed but usually for detailed design and/or to establish a "due-diligence" record to protect against any future unpleasantness.

What might be an example of an enterprise's use of mathematical models? I don't quite understand.

Suppose you are starting an auto insurance company and decide that premiums paid in should be about three times expected payouts. The mathematics for setting premiums is then just a constant multiplier of three times the expected payouts, *a* simple mathematical model. But suppose that operating costs are excessive for very small claims so the model is modified from three to two-and-a-half for customers willing to pay the first $2,000 of their claim. That works well, but you also are losing money on customers whose accidents generate claims over $300,000. So you stop writing policies with coverage above that level. Further analysis of the model also shows that young male teenagers are a higher risk, so a surcharge is added to certain age ranges. Other model changes indicate that premium variations by zip code are advantageous.

Pardon me, but that sounds pretty rudimentary, cluttered but simple; It's just arithmetic.

Right. Of course, the actuary is using some fancy statistical formulas to set premiums per customer in order to assure the aggregate premium figures for next year. But up to this point the models can be analyzed with a hand calculator.

Then at the next board meeting, a stockholder asks whether another year as bad as last year's will jeopardize the stock's value. Company security guards deal with the immediate problem. But for next year, a contingency cushion is clearly required. The model can then be expanded to indicate each year's extra premium necessary to build a protective surplus so that the probability of bankruptcy from an actuarial fluctuation is less than perhaps 1 percent. Delays in claim processing might suggest a queuing model to help reorganize the processing flow and so forth.

Interesting, but it raises a paradox for me. Won't most people with autos prefer 100 percent coverage above $300,000, even at a higher premium? Why would anyone buy the policy you've described?

Out of ignorance, I suppose. The few customers who understand the protection limits of their policy don't think about it, or don't believe they will ever need protection at a "catastrophic" $300,000 level. Then there's the uncertainty of risk mitigation's value versus price in the purchaser's mind. The company's less-than-informative advertising focuses on how secure you and your family will feel with the insurance carrier looking after you, and how effortless and enjoyable the claims settlement process will be if needed.

Interesting. I gather that you use mathematical models to test prospective control or policy decisions as well as to monitor how the current decisions are working.

Yes, so you needn't inadvertently lose 20 percent of your market share on a bad idea if you can test it on the mathematical model first. And often, in setting up the model and acquiring the data, some entirely new idea is inspired.

In large organizations with many transactions, the mathematics must be formidable.

Fortunately, computers handle the repetitive calculations once the model is set up. These days, advanced mathematical knowledge is not always needed. Knowledge of what the math and the model can and can't do, plus understanding of what the computer software is capable of and requires as input, is enough to at worst retain and work with specialists.

Is that all?

Pretty much. Of course, a validation/audit subsystem or process is needed to assure the accuracy and authenticity of the model, the software, and the calculation's results. For some applications, a qualitative, "Does it make sense? Is it reasonable?" type of judgment will suffice. If malevolent intrusion is a concern, such as fraud in voting machines or credit card identity theft, the models are necessarily complex and dynamic, and under constant scrutiny.

So what's the actual process of engineering a system?

Well, every system has a life-cycle. First it is conceptualized. Then some stakeholders agree on the performance requirements, structure, and resource acquisitions. Next, engineers design and produce it, test its actual behavior, install it, train personnel, and eventually monitor system operations. Once the system is operational, misjudgments in performance requirement trade-offs, design, production, performance, and utilization may emerge. As necessary and ongoing "improvements" are made, the system may subsequently be upgraded and eventually retired. Systems engineers get involved in each of these life-cycle phases.

To sum up, once explained, the basics of systems concepts are intuitively obvious, even anticlimactic. But, as is true of many "simple" concepts, they shouldn't be dismissed too quickly. They are powerful in breadth and depth and functionality. Much human behavior that is ludicrous and dangerous could be examined, and some even corrected, if analyzed as complex systems that involve multiple stakeholders.

Most edifying, and on that note might we proceed to dinner? I'll meet you there as scheduled.

Oops! We have a one-hour delay because of a reservation glitch. Is that OK, or shall I find us another restaurant?

No problem. It gives us another opportunity for more e-mail chatting if you have time right now. Actually it may facilitate our dealing with some details rather than trying to do so in your lovely restaurant.

That's fine. Let's proceed.

SESSION 26

Your comments about systems being ubiquitous and system thinking and tools being generic; I see now what that means more than I did. Systems engineers must be greatly admired and respected by the general public.

Well no, not especially. What we do isn't rocket science—well some of it is. It's certainly not brain surgery. Most of it isn't life-threatening, except to us if we make a mistake. ☺ Anyone who can be comfortable with a systematic perspective and has patience can do much of what we do. Here is an example from my own experience.

That would help and you mentioned mistakes. What kinds of mistakes are common?

I had some ideas for improving the design of mammography machines for breast cancer screening. So I conducted a patent search, attracted some venture capital—easy to do, given the projected market demand. Then I developed the business plan. But at some point an inner-voice told me to reassess the situation. Who are the stakeholders, what are their goals, strengths and weaknesses, and what's the overall situation?

Interesting. Shouldn't you have done those things in reverse order?

I suppose, but the creative process isn't always orderly, and everything connects to everything else. It's a system, remember. The main thing is be sure you cover all the bases before committing all the resources.

What did you discover?

I learned that despite the enticing market-growth projections, mammography is really no better than palpation as a screening device for reducing breast cancer mortality rates. In addition, accumulated radiation exposure from periodic mammogram screening is probably as likely to cause a cancer as is the likelihood of detecting a cancer via mammography.

What did you do, sketch a stakeholder diagram?

Sarcasm noted. Actually, I did do a flow chart and spreadsheet or two that helped confirm the situation. The paradox I and my investors needed to understand was the vigorous growth of the mammography market for equipment, clinical usage, and associated litigation in view of the above facts. The detailed diagram guided by an informal survey confirmed that:

- fear drives the at-risk patient to demand action;

- treatment centers and practitioners want to satisfy patients and stockholders by responding proactively within "standard of care" constraints;

- equipment-makers support mammography, and prosper and promote their products vigorously;

- detection screening is intrinsically difficult, partly because cancer still isn't well-understood; and

- the equipment and demographics of screened populations change faster than reliable research results can accrue, disseminate, and influence clinical practice.

What about keepers of the "standard of care?"

Eligible and experienced committee members often emerge from one of the stakeholder institutions. Their biases, the peer harmony pressures for compromise, and deadlines to produce consensus tend to shape any recommendations, especially in the absence of solid research information.

I can see the value of detailed stakeholder analyses here. What did you do?

I stared at the ceiling for quite awhile. Then I decided to read a lot, from which I learned enough to know what questions to ask. Then I bought lunch in exchange for enlightenment from a series of doctors and nurses, revised my business plan, and rather than returning unused funds to the investors, persuaded them to agree to the new plan.

Which is ...?

Since self-examination by palpation seems to work but is often not properly done, I designed a glove plus computer chip using "smart skin" developed for robotic hands as input to a computer system. This improves hand sensitivity substantially and provides computer-printed palpation results that can be compared for month-to-month trends.

Sounds great. How can I invest?

Very funny. We're in field trials at the moment. If they're successful and the patent situation is favorable, I hope to license the program to a medical equipment distributor.

Why don't you do it yourself?

While I might have enjoyed the field testing computer simulations of the manufacture, sales, and distribution functions convinced me to license it. Before making this decision I looked at innumerable variables and their mutual dependency, including:

- the legal costs of acquiring a solid patent position and defending it;

- the necessary criteria for selecting the best equipment distributor;

- whether to partner with an overseas manufacturer;

- the optimal process for working through the regulatory jungle knowing that the established "mammography bureaucracy" would not prove helpful; and

- the marketing campaign that would best educate and convince clinicians that the product would help rather than hurt their practice.

Aren't these the standard sort of business decisions that non-systems people make all the time?

Absolutely, but because these decisions almost all interrelate, especially when starting a new enterprise with a new technology, it is especially valuable to be able to conduct a systems study. Much of the analysis can be done in a simple manner but some require a full-blown computer based dynamic simulation.

How's our time? I'm starting to get hungry.

Me too, but we have a few more minutes. Tell me more about your planet. How did your planet deal with the same sort of grim challenges we face here? Did you avoid large wealth/

poverty disparities? Is your working middle class a vital socio-economic stabilizer and if so, is unemployment a problem? What do you do about loose cannons like Timothy McVeigh when potent weapons are so available? Do you use a coalition of national governments to coordinate intelligence and fight terrorism?

These are the right questions, of course, and I'll mention some of what we do. But let's both keep in mind that differences in our respective planets and peoples may preclude duplicating our solutions to solve Earth's problems.

Yes, yes, but it's a good place to work from.

OK. Where I come from, human development is carefully orchestrated to maintain strong bonds with one's family and community. Family and extended family members are punished along with any law-breaker. Justice is swift; appeals are limited and errors in favor of the state are tolerated "for the greater good." They are few because of our advanced forensic science and surveillance networks, of course. Individuality without designated family bonds is taboo and subject to criminal action—a recluse such as your Mr. McVeigh would simply not be permitted.

Crime against the state is monitored without regard to privacy. We have layered safeguards which protect due process and which guard against misuse of our surveillance networks. As a systems engineer, I'm sure you would be quite impressed. Polygraph testing and truth-extraction are highly developed, widely utilized, and accepted as screening techniques. Thus the threat of WMD and sociopolitical or culture-based turmoil is avoided, community life is cohesive and rewarding, the emotional security is gratifying, with fears and self-doubts quickly dealt with by family, community, or state, all backed by enlightened medication as appropriate. With a robotic work force, there is time for strong national, community, and personal relations.

It sounds like our tribalism, only secular, more hierarchical and controlled, I guess because your telecommunication and surveillance technologies are more advanced than ours. Do you like living there? Would I?

Yes, I very much like living there. I believe you would also, after a period of adjustment—certainly your grandchildren would. ☺

It's difficult to explain relationships because your species is saturated with inherited values, instincts, and behaviors that we replaced long ago. Sociopolitical and cultural harmony are given great value and attention, essential to keep our planet functioning. Toward that end, educational achievement, information access, and political influence are keyed to what is akin to security clearance levels here.

The monogamous relationship which you Earthlings devised during prehistoric times served several vital evolutionary purposes. We don't need that custom on our planet, certainly not any more. Compared to Earthlings, you might say that our sexual relations are almost bland, lacking the intensity and urgency to establish or maintain self-esteem in physical or psychological dimensions, or even vicarious immortality. The trauma of sexual rejection or constraint just isn't there. Private or postponed sex is permitted but not encouraged. With effective contraception and disease control, the rationale for most of your sexual taboos carries no weight for us.

Similarly, the urge to procreate—part of your primitive legacy, has *no great potency for us. Because the state has taken over the conception and early nurturing functions, the logistics inconvenience, and sociopolitical stress are avoided. It obviates the possibility of intense jealousies and romance, which compete and perhaps endan-*

ger society's cohesiveness and substantive agenda. Accordingly, the nuclear family's role has far less prominence than I see here.

It sounds like all your emotions are muted. I don't think I'd like that.

We feel some things very strongly and others not. For example, the sanctity of life is much stronger at home than here; taking a human life is almost unimaginable for us. On the other hand, anyone with a strong adherence to property rights would for us connote low self-esteem and the need for therapy. The idea of interest paid on a loan or dividends on an investment would seem perverted. At the same time, the events of birth and death are neither celebrated nor feared as they are here. Leading a life of tranquility, service, openness, humor (very important), self-development, and affection—these factors make birth and death not as traumatic as it seems to be for you Earthlings.

That's helpful input. I know we've talked about some of this before but it is so exotic, that it helps to review it.

Of course, and a final reminder: On my planet, the backdrop for all this includes the consistent availability of adequate food, health care, education, and security. So there is little need for demons, tribal competition, and conflict. Survival of the fittest loses potency when everyone survives. It's a relaxed, benign, civilized, supportive atmosphere. Rules and taboos are few, but enforcement is swift and potent when a violation or its potential occurs.

You just mentioned food. It's time to go get ours. See you at the restaurant?

Right-o.

SESSION 27

We need to talk. Are you there? I know you're there; I can feel it. Look, I apologize for everything. I couldn't have known that the restaurant's reservation delay was caused by their kitchen fire, or that the residual smoke smell would be intolerable, or that they would pack up our dinner to go and that taking it to my apartment would lead to what it did. And your leaving without waking me or leaving a note ... please say something; I know you're there.

OK, I guess that's not much of an apology, but I am truly sorry and admit to having been the primary activist in breaking our abstinence pledge. I'll also admit that in retrospect the pledge was unrealistic for me and would be even more unrealistic, looking to the future. Once you and I are in the same room, well ... please talk to me.

I can't right now. Let's try to get some work done.

OK. Good idea, I suppose. Let's see....

Back to Timothy McVeigh, al-Qaeda members and those other loose-cannon problems we touched on. As a systems designer I know that defective components can occur anywhere in the system, so using failure analysis the crucial components are identified and "best practices" are built into fail-safe configurations. It sounds like just as we attend to the component and subsystem level, you do the same when addressing the potential perpetrator, including his/her access to information, materials, and processes. As McVeigh's behavior became more bizarre, his family, being individually and severally responsible for his mental health and attitudes, would be obligated to blow the whistle for therapy or incarceration, as appropriate.

That's right, and as I said before, hermits are not permitted. In addition, everyone receives polygraph-type testing, interviews, and counseling by non-family professionals, often and unannounced. Some of your friends would be horrified at this intrusive loss of privacy, but they would be more horrified to see a Timothy McVeigh armed with the modern weapons that are available to anyone. Where a family's or small community's self-policing is unreliable, the alternative is maintaining weapons-free zones and controlled, connecting corridors with constant surveillance—much as you manage your military bases or prisons.

With regard to the weaponry, we don't worry about nuclear; that's easily dealt with by sensor surveillance networks. Chemical weapons, although easy to mask and deploy, don't cause widespread devastation, and a potential perpetrator with the training, technology, and intention is easily detected with the polygraph and surveillance techniques. Incidentally, our polygraph technology is far more unobtrusive yet sophisticated and error-proof than yours, thanks to a miniscule chip implanted at birth. The remaining difficulty pertains to bacteriological weapons. We control source materials and technical information rigorously. Those with technical expertise are monitored closely and certified periodically.

Is that pretty much it?

Not quite. Above the familial level we have community education and surveillance programs. Our permitted religious and sectarian organizations are required to include indoctrination, which reinforces the sanctity of life and frequently reminds us of the rewards and punishments received by adherence to and disruption of the status quo.

We'd find it difficult to rely on the nuclear family as the first line of defense against a McVeigh type threat. Our poorest people can't afford consistent family and community relations. Our affluent people utilize family life for early nurturing of children, but then attach great importance to those children becoming independent of family. We expect the nuclear family to be independent of its neighbor families and the community to a large extent. Even when heads of families are overprotective and try to cling to their children, the result is to drive the children away, toward independence. Protection of the elderly is largely left to the state. So except for a few religious groups, we no longer have a viable mutually supportive network of nuclear families to achieve what you seem to have.

Unlike your planet, mine protects and improves the sociopolitical systems within bounds that protect it, not as a white elephant but as a creative, growing process. As in other orderly, stable cultures, we withhold employment, marriage, and acknowledgement of births and deaths from deviants. Few, but strong, taboos are clearly defined, triggering ostracism, which is real, frightening, and painful rather than geographical. We have randomly selected task forces with complete access to everything; their unscheduled spot-checks and reporting processes are carefully designed for maximum transparency and dissemination. These are very useful, too.

What prevents a family from becoming a terrorist sleeper cell with its own agenda?

As I've mentioned before, the loose-cannon threat is dealt with by not permitting loners; everyone must be part of a family and the extended family is responsible for all its members, with substantial rewards and punishments for breaches in that responsibility. The backup is unobtrusive but provides constant surveillance by what you might think of as advanced, wireless surveillance.

If it's part of a network, we'll pick up on them quickly by eavesdropping and sting operations. The techniques are similar to yours, except that our advanced technology provides more precise, timely intelligence with a combination of tightly programmed and monitored equipment and agents. Yes, it's an all-pervasive police program with penetration and corruption safeguards you wouldn't believe, yet virtually invisible and unobtrusive.

I sense that you disapprove, focusing on what my people seem to have given up relative to yours. And I grant you that in "simpler times" we also had some laissez-faire, charming attributes comparable to those of your societies. On the other hand, when you look at it in context, even if our planet's maturation had been identical to yours, the roles of men and women, the structure of families, and how they connect to their communities had to change. It was one pattern when the family's main concern was not getting eaten by tigers or neighboring tribes, but completely another when the male transitioned from hunter-gatherer-warrior to employee and husband. Can't you visualize a world where the "breadwinner" gets his bread without working forty hours per week and the soccer-mom is free to have a life beyond constant child care?

It still sounds dehumanizing and radically controlling.

I understand how you feel. I'm not doing very well explaining it. You are used to a particular lifestyle and sociopolitical context, so the compromises between the individual's and the state's prerogatives here have become almost invisible to you. Look, your planet has had innumerable wars. Most of them were a natural conse-quence of your civilization's evolution and as such, killed people and rearranged boundaries, but didn't disrupt the underlying movement toward a more enlightened civilization. But now, in modern times you've had a few, what might be called unnatural, maybe even unnecessary, wars; wars caused by individual leaders rather than irreconcilable or inflammatory circumstances. Those wars are particularly disruptive because there is no intrinsic reason for them within the society that is therefore caught unaware. They are not only disruptive in the usual sense but they destroy and then recreate very different fundamental and broad conditions of your economic and sociopolitical characteristics—the proverbial para-digm shift.

Which of our many wars do you have in mind?

Well, some recent examples include World War II, the Cold War, and now what your politicians euphemistically call "countert-errorism." With quite different values, motives, and intentions, the various instigators shared only the ineptitude in predicting the out-come of their respective conflicts and probably the conviction that their enemy had started it all. However, the planet's civilizations would never be the same again after these wars ended. So don't be so resistant to the notion that your society, in its remaining years, will never again be as it was.

From your description of life in a stable society, once WMD are available, frankly, it sounds terribly complicated, intrusive, and constraining for the loyal citizenry. I'm dubious that we could ever do all that here. Culture in every successful country on Earth has individual privacy and independence as a virtual hallmark. Maybe I didn't understand your cryptic sketch. Please tell me more.

Look, let's get serious. You have inner-privacy; you Earthlings are adept at denial, selective perception, selective memory, self-deception, and delegation of responsibility, to name a few. But your outer privacy is porous via high resolution satellite surveillance, spy software, bugs of all sorts, and ubiquitous, barely discernable cameras. So you're overdue for rethinking the situation. Privacy is becoming obsolete as a protective defense, so think about other ways of self-protection against the fears and actual damage that privacy used to protect you from.

All these safeguards sound prohibitively labor-intensive. I can't even visualize it.

Labor-intensive? In my world, robots do all the work, leaving lots of humans available to help. You're moving in that direction right now.

It also seems outlandishly expensive and politically unattainable.

Expensive and politically unattainable? Visualize a world in which the affluent, politically powerful elite perceive their self-interest, even survival, as contingent on assuring equal opportunity and justice for every element of society, made credible and actionable by steadfast morality supported by long-term self-interest. That can happen, once the society's members believe they can attain more within the system than by destroying it.

So, have I destroyed our "system," that is friendship?

No, not at all. But I need some time to think. As a systems engineer, you will appreciate that for someone having grown up in a culture which is "systematic" at all societal levels down to family and individual, I might need some time to process the incongruities—dare I say paradoxes?, within our friendship. Shall we continue our work? Same time tomorrow?

Yes, great!

SESSION 28

Look, I admit I don't totally grasp what's going on here. I've been looking at your Declaration of Independence and wondering why people here attach such importance to a document that starts with "We hold these truths to be self-evident ... " And then "... endowed by their creator with certain inalienable rights ... created equal ... life, liberty and the pursuit of happiness?"

Why are you confused? That's a clear, straightforward, revered document.

Well, if the truths are self-evident, what's the big fuss about the document that writes them down? And "creator"? I thought this was a secular government. Also, nobody is ever created equal to anyone else, thanks to some rather important prenatal distinctions. Even if everyone was created equal, there would still be inequalities of opportunity afterward. Then to claim that everyone has the right to life, liberty, and the pursuit of happiness ... well, on this increasingly crowded planet, it all sounds like an advertisement for selling weapons, since every person's pursuit of happiness, life, and liberty will conflict with others.

From this and other documents, it seems that when a document or person talks about intrinsic rights, it's usually to compel "the people" to do something they are otherwise disinclined to do. Also, the writers don't seem to differentiate the fundamental rights very well from rights attached to what they believe are necessary for the society. The United Nations' particular compilation in the Universal Declaration of Human Rights includes not just rights but some approaches to securing them, like unionizing, and some hallmarks of having them, like education, mobility, and privacy. But semantic nitpicks aside; the document doesn't include a UN commitment to securing these rights! So why bother?

It's not like when Newton says that mass will accelerate proportional to the applied force. The laws of motion will make it happen without our having to do anything. Labor leaders telling workers of their rights first want the workers to join the union, re-elect the union leadership, pay their dues, and strike if the union negotiators aren't well-treated by management. Lawyers and politicians telling potential clients and constituents of their rights simply want to be retained, ostensibly to fight for those rights.

You are one cynical extraterrestrial!

Thank you. I gather that's usually a pejorative, but in this context, thanks anyway. I think our conversation is clouded by our respective backgrounds. Specifically, every viable society must balance rights and constraints of the individual versus the state. Your planet has been completing a phase of high individual autonomy and mortality rates; the classic competitive resource-scarcity phase. Now as you transition into global integration of your socioeconomic and security institutions, mortality rates are less resource dependent but more security dependent. During this transition, the particular clutch of human rights you've enjoyed is no longer assured, nor espe-

cially relevant. I've grown up in a world that's completed the transition you are just entering.

I don't much like what I'm hearing.

Look at "privacy of the individual and transparency of government." Americans talk and act as if that's a holy mantra rather than simply a trade-off mechanism for protecting citizens and stabilizing institutions. But when terrorists are running around, trying to kill people and destroy those institutions, wouldn't you prefer more transparency of the individual and privacy of the government in the interest of survival? There's nothing intrinsically valuable about privacy; it's just a mechanism, one of many.

Well, I don't know….

Apparently. Look, I'm trying to help you. Your civilization, America in particular, has been enjoying military and economic successes which engender complacency and devotion to the trouble-free status quo. This encourages your hedonism and the dumb-down of leadership, values, institutions, and the consequent policies. Publics are neutralized through the combination of deception, deflection, fatalism, myopia, and self-imposed ignorance. The few with insights are reclusive, inarticulate, or bereft of pulpit or power. Behavior is regulated by fear/greed, superstition, taboos, and "we/they" antagonisms. But those modern savages dancing around bonfires aren't waving spears; those are Uzis and laptops. I'd say you have real management challenges to stabilize this planet like mine.

Well, I'm not so sure we want to even go there. It sounds like you carry pragmatism and survival to such extremes that aesthetics, idealism, human spirit, even ethics and morality, are subordinated to global survival. In the process, people get hurt. I feel that you have hurt me with your little deceptive masquer-

ade. Maybe it's time for us to call a halt to our so-called collaboration.

*Yes, perhaps we should. But first, please understand that it was
your confounded systems methodology that brought us to where we
are.*

What are you saying?

*My anatomy maps and flowcharts of this planet as a system were
easy to produce and illuminated several insights for me. A predomi-
nant one was that the system components—in particular, personal
relationships,* have *much more influence on system behavior than
on our planet. And as you preach, especially in the counterterrorism
example, it is vital to understand the characteristics of components,
systems, and subsystems; how the inputs affect the respective outputs.*

So what does that have to do with what happened between
us?

*Do I need to spell it out for you? You Earthlings are so preoccu-
pied with sex, not just animalistic reproduction but orgasm,
orgasm, orgasm! It seems to run everything either directly or as the
background music in product design, films, magazines, music …
everything. In contrast, on my planet, as I've explained before, with
our sensory implants and sperm-egg banks, well … I for one had no
direct experience and as you have mentioned more than once, some
experiences defy description. To continue your prescribed systems
analysis inquiry, I felt it necessary to acquire the experience.*

Weird, but understandable, I suppose. But why me?

*Contrary to what you may be thinking, I was not interested in
embarking on a statistical sampling of sex with Earthlings; one such
experience would suffice. Almost every woman's magazine lists criteria for partner selection: prior experience, strong physical attraction,
knowing and feeling safe with a partner through prior communication and common interests. As I understood it, privacy is required*

for satisfactory sexual encounters. Interruption by angry spouses, curious children, or house pets dilutes the interaction. You were the ideal candidate.

OK, that makes sense. But why didn't you tell me?

Several considerations, but please don't get angry. I'm feeling quite vulnerable right now, as some of the magazine articles predict. I didn't think you would, or could, knowingly transition from colleague to serving as my exploratory research lab in the single encounter that I had in mind.

Single encounter? We were together a solid seventy-two hours that first time! And if that was just research, you gave a very convincing performance of something quite different and evoked feelings in me that ... never mind.

Yes, well, I can only explain how things started with my intention of a single—and believe me, I hadn't the slightest notion of what was to follow, totally unexpected, the sudden intensity of affection, communion, the compelling desire to share these blissful feelings with others ... with my partner, a child, family, or community.

Me too, actually. And then?

I'd expected those euphoric feelings were biologically based and would recede within a day or two at most. So I felt unperturbed at the suggestion of our dining in your apartment. Obviously, I was somewhat mistaken. I'm doing all the talking. Please, your turn.

At this moment, I feel disoriented, overwhelmed, relieved, confused, and ecstatic. I'm used to dissecting things and you're integrating them for me. Amazing! I must ask if you are OK, where you are at this moment, whether you feel we can keep working together. But mostly, are you OK?

Yes, I think so, and I'd favor trying to continue working together, at least for a little while. Where am I at this moment? Here are some fragmentary speculations; not research findings:

I begin to understand the tribe's interventions with taboos, recognition, rewards, and punishments around a couple's physical relationship. That's because it can be so potent as to threaten or support the tribe substantially.

How so?

For me at least, there's a strong desire to share the euphoria, including a powerful desire to "nest," both with my partner, potential progeny, and with my community. That nesting is some combination of enjoying, nurturing, and protecting, which I feel can be passive or extremely active. Fearing the latter, I now understand better why your governments get involved in "women's issues."

What about the male?

Here, I'm less sure, but in sharing and observing your responses; their intensity and quality begin to explain the man's willingness to endure an intensely demeaning and dangerous life, whether in combat, at work, or at home, just in order to acquire or perpetuate a successful relationship—and how destructive its absence can be. So I'd imagine that the tribal leadership must have a correspondingly strong interest in harnessing, directing, or encapsulating some of this male energy for its own agendas of survival or advancement.

It had not occurred to me how strong the sociopolitical linkage to sex must be here. It also explains why some of your people would reject the "prescribed" heterosexual, committed relationship altogether, reacting to the sociopolitical pressures encountered.

Fascinating. What about for you, more personally?

Well, it's so different from anything I'd experienced. It's like going on a totally unfamiliar journey which suddenly brings me to my home, to myself.

Maybe I can explain it better in terms of my music. Your chamber music seems to feature quartets and trios; at home we do more with duets. And yes, the crescendos are outstanding and memorable. But between those crescendos, the communication and communion of mood, of affection, of occasional solo passages supported by my partner, these are treasured, gratifying experiences also. Without these andante passages incidentally, the crescendos wouldn't be nearly as intense or meaningful, at least to this woman.

Tell me, for a male, is it all about crescendos? That's certainly the impression I get from walking around.

I don't know. I haven't taken a survey. But for me, before we'd met, I would have answered both yes and no. I think that if left alone while growing up, I'd only have been interested in "crescendos." But I wasn't left alone. My family, friends, and various role models "programmed" me for the stereotypic roles of crescendo-seeker, then spouse-parent-provider, none of which included the non-crescendo music you describe. That, I've only experienced very recently ... with you and you must know that I love it ... and you.

Same time tomorrow?

Yes, all right.

SESSION 29

We've agreed to not complicate our work with chatter about our personal interaction, but I keep wondering about the unprecedented intensity of the feelings we've generated. Is it because humans on our respective planets are different in ways that trigger this intense, interpersonal chemistry, or are you and I unique in that way with each other, irrespective of our origins in the cosmos?

I wonder about that too. And I've also been apprehensive that your people and mine may be different in important ways which affect transferability of some of our solutions to some of your problems. So I've been out and about again, trying to understand you Earthlings, focusing on human behavior rather than sociopolitical and global characteristics. And I've deliberately stayed with you Americans, convinced that despite your anachronistic institutions, your affluence and culture, such as it is, offer the most hopeful triggers for moving ahead.

I'm delighted to hear that you're "out and about." I hope you are being careful about where you go and what you ask the locals. I don't want you to be at risk.

That's touching and appreciated. I'm concerned about your survival here, too. Perhaps you'd consider coming home with me? We'll talk about that another time. Here are some observations about your people; hopefully less naïve than my earlier comments on arrival.

- *The reluctance to defer gratification, let alone to take risks today for future benefits, is pervasive. It may be the greatest obstacle to implementing survival initiatives for this planet. It is reinforced by the many products and services that are configured for short-term gratification, be it entertainment and recreation, health care, or consumer credit.*

- *Denial of mortality is pervasive, helped by cosmetics and plastic surgery, wardrobe, diet, and exercise. Sick people are encapsulated and/or ostracized. They get blamed for reminding healthy people that immortality is a myth. All this tension and fear provokes a need to insist that something be done—which accounts for many of the useless, often harmful medical tests and drugs.*

- *Offsetting this "Do something" imperative, there is fatalism, a tenet of most religions which is also popular. It tends to create large families, too poor to threaten the leadership, and it excuses adherents for not striving harder or feeling responsible. This works best if feelings of inadequacy are reinforced via prayers of the "unworthy to the almighty," esoteric language and intimidating houses of worship.*

- *Earthlings are drawn to the idea of an afterlife. Religions that offer an appealing, tangible afterlife are popular, conferring hope for the future and acceptance of the present because it's tempo-*

rary. The powerful elite embrace whatever preserves the status quo, so it's a win-win situation.

- *Earthlings exhibit a strong tendency to discount past gains, probably an evolved trait of survivors. Those who rested on their laurels or stopped to count their blessings got eaten by the tigers. In addition, Earthlings' insatiable hunger for self-esteem reinforcement may perpetuate discontent, ambition, and challenge to the status quo. A truly stable society may never be possible if the species' propensity is to always indiscriminately strive for more, especially if at the expense of others.*

- *Symbols substitute for reality in many aspects of the culture. Buying a sports car implies virility. Redecorating the kitchen means being nurtured and loved. Vesting of stock options signifies that the recipient is a fine human being, in good standing with God as well as the SEC.*

- *Earthlings find comfort in feeling superior to and different from another ethnic or religious group. It avoids having to feel responsible for their welfare; it provides demons when needed.*

- *Misperceptions and misconceptions are most often self-induced myopia and/or selective perception. Such <u>views</u> can be subordinated very quickly when enlightened self-interest intervenes. Feelings take longer to change and vestiges of genetic imprinting take a very long time. These distinctions can be important in devising realistic conceptual models for analyzing survival initiatives.*

The thrust of your observations seems to be that we Earthlings aren't fond of perceiving and accepting reality. I can't disagree with what you're saying. I have friends who act as if they believe reality to be overrated. My children probably have bumper stickers or t-shirts expressing that sentiment.

Do you disagree?

Well, of course! No, wait a minute. I guess if I'm in a safe environment in which no harm is being done, I can conjure up virtual realities that are much more gratifying than the real thing, certainly for the moment. But maybe not ... I guess I'm not so sure anymore.

Good comment. You have far more depth than I'd imagined. You could have been a musicologist. ☺

Thanks, but I can barely handle the euphoria evoked by a well-designed and functioning engineering system. How could I deal with the intangible, indefinable aesthetics of music?

I'd be honored and delighted to accept the challenge of showing you the way, just as you have shown me. Let's get back to work.

Summing up my observations I listed above, your planet's survival traits have been successful in a resource-scarce ecology. But now in your resource-abundant ecology, transitioning is a serious problem. Earthlings might start with breaking the annoying habit of looking on the bright side or not looking at all. Fortunately, you humans are far more versatile than you appear. Your behavioral attributes are almost identical to ours, and we made it. So if you can figure out how to rebalance this outdated culture and its institutions synergistically, you just might make it too.

I'm in need of a break to process all this. Tomorrow, same time?

Yes, that's fine.

SESSION 30

You asked where I am. I'm on two tracks at the moment. I want to see how we might connect these behavioral characteristics to our global survival issues. But more urgently, I want to understand better how or if our personal interactions relate.

Fair enough. In thinking and rethinking what has transpired with us, let me first say that the degree to which I could feel an intensity, almost ecstasy from our physical interaction, well—it was delightful, a revelation. But it also left me angry.

Angry? How so?

A hoax, perhaps inadvertent, has been perpetrated on my people. Our sensory chip is completely satisfying, but the tranquility conferred comes at the price of never experiencing the peak ecstasy; not knowing of the possibility or the choice ... am I making sense?

Yes you are. Do you think it's a calculated, political control scheme?

Good question and one I intend to look in to when I get home. The more general and fundamental issue is the degree to which we ET's and Earthlings alike, deliberately risk the "feel good" comforting reinforcement of conformity from our genetic programming and

external socialization against those peak moments of ecstasy ema-
nating purely from the self, uninhibited by all that other program-
ming. It might explain why the orgasm may be seen as not worth it;
a threat to overall equanimity, either at the personal, interpersonal,
or sociopolitical level. The rewards from taking that particular risk
could induce reconsideration of other risk-reward decisions; a
frightening, possibly dangerous prospect in itself. So I'm not taking
a position here, just explaining to myself why something I find sur-
prisingly delightful, many others choose to reject.

Any other surprises?

Just that a strong emotional bond must form if the participating
partner is consistently supportive, feels honored and appreciative of
the exposed vulnerability intrinsic to the act—as I sense from you.

You've given me a great deal to think about and to integrate
into my own new insights. An immediate one is that I've always
perceived the nuclear family system as evolved primarily from
adaptations to its external inputs. You're causing me to consider
that the couple's bonding could be a more potent energizer;
depending of course on their basic compatibility as well as how
their relationship is formed initially and nurtured thereafter. I
need to think about that, plus the filters and fantasies we all use
to enhance or insulate our partner interactions. That may make
more sense when I've digested your amazing comments. Meanwhile, let's proceed.

You've just mentioned the probable importance of the couple's
bonding compatibility, and formation. My impression is that your
planet's current problems and future solutions relate directly to the
strength and quality of these relationships. These relationships ide-
ally should be the durable yet adaptable components, that is, the
building blocks of your survival systems, certainly while your insti-
tutions and culture are undergoing wrenching realignments ahead.

Maybe you're right. And therefore?

Well for one thing, as I study your Internet, I see that you don't have even a rudimentary version of our Partner Selection Optimizer! As a result, there is no mechanism for even injecting, let alone balancing, societal and community imperatives in partner selection. It's a totally chaotic, inefficient process of finding, meeting, and experiencing potential rejection by a seemingly endless number of candidates. The time required to "network" with people you don't like in hopes of being introduced to people you will like, or to "surf" the beach, the bars, the fundraisers, the Internet, is inordinate—not to mention the inevitably battered egos and budgets. Yuck! I really don't understand it, but I'd wager that you have lots of empirical data that might help enlighten me.

Well data, yes. But the hardest problem is the need to package and market oneself while striving to minimize the risk of rejection. For the neophytes, it's a demeaning, exhausting process that causes the participant to suppress her/his inner-identity and critical thinking. The more experienced, scarred players carefully limit their expectations, hopes, and dreams while protecting vulnerabilities—which almost guarantees a bland, disappointing result. Males particularly may focus on sex-without-involvement, while females settle for a presentable escort and loneliness antidote.

But why are there so many unproductive first-meeting rejections?

Most encounters fail to fit within the preconceived "acceptability windows." In the aftermath of my divorce I could see that in any new relationship I wanted lots of freedom, but also a sense of shelter and familiarity. That left a very narrow opening for a relationship. I recognize it in others as almost too much or too little similarity to a parent or to a previous lover, or too much or too little affinity with the local taboos and culture.

The first-meeting ritual itself is a sequence of mutual observations. Very occasionally, one of these preliminary encounters
leads to continuity and deepening of a relationship. The "glue"
that perpetuates and strengthens the process seems to have
many different modalities. Sometimes it is a physical or mental
attraction, or collaboration in work, recreation, or psychic reinforcement; maybe an attraction to the other person's family or
sports car.

*I suspect that if the relationship moves to a permanent commit-
ment, almost invariably, major reassessments must occur. The previous perceptions and misperceptions must now be readjusted,
transforming the entire conceptual framework of the relationship.*

I think that's right. Marriage, augmented by the advent of
children, replaces peer pressures with even more potent constraints. The constraints of limited time, sleep, and income,
combined with family and community needs, stringently limit
opportunities for the relationship to freshen and grow.

*That would seem to explain many of the bizarre behaviors I'm
observing: ubiquitous infidelity, rape, domestic violence, and family
disintegration. Unfortunately, the widespread suppression of conflict or disconnects left unresolved must create the proverbial "lives
of quiet desperation."*

Yes. Examples? One of my friends from a smoothly running
but loveless family started dating; equipped with a standard set
of needs, fears, and taboos. Poor Chris, she projected a tranquil,
warm, and integrated exterior. But inside, she could only be
relaxed enough for intimacy if the relationship contained some
prominent, insurmountable blockage to permanency. So she
successively committed to and then parted from a married man,
a lesbian, an emotionally closed lothario, a much older man,

then a young rabbi—she is an African-American Baptist, by the way.

Another friend, George, was deeply committed but ultimately rejected by his lover of many years. In the aftermath, his capacity or willingness to love declined, leaving only the demeanor of a caring, sensitive nature. He was very appealing but very damaging to trusting women since his true agenda, hidden even from himself, was to maximize the number of new seductions with minimum conversation and certainly no personal involvement. The motto, "So many women, so little time," was not printed on his t–shirt, but it was tattooed over his heart.

Then there was Herb. I don't know where he is now. But I recall one very pungent conversation. His girlfriend since high school and through college became pregnant. They married. He worked two jobs, attempted graduate school, had things interrupted by military service, returned, had more children, worked more overtime, and got more promotions. In monotone, but with a memorable intensity about his eyes, he recited how many millions he'd had to earn in order to support and then launch family members, while living in the expensive cities necessitated by his work.

While admired and envied by all for his ebullience, diligence, and good luck, he confided to me that he saw things quite differently. He attributed his apparent success primarily to the commitment he'd made to smile—not only in the face of adversity but even in the face of insult. Demeaned by skeptical in-laws, narcissistic college professors, the autocratic football coach, egotistical bosses, military superiors, investors, union negotiators, corporate attorneys, bank lending officers, IRS auditors, shareholders, his teenage children—"Even your wife?"

I'd interrupted. "Well, not overtly," he said, "until she found her tennis coach and divorce lawyer. My fault I suppose. But with everyone else in my life taking bites from my carcass, it was hard to feel validation and strokes from a wife, attached to me by the marriage contract and financial dependence. I know from my work that just because a contractor smiles, it doesn't mean he thinks I'm terrific. So subconsciously I may have discounted her overtures as obligatory. We never really talked about things like that."

For an Earthling, especially for an engineer, you seem very aware of human behavior in relationships. How did that happen?

Thank you. I think it started in freshman chemistry. My lab partner became my first friend at college. We had some fantastic, soul-searching discussions. I was the first American she'd been able to talk with seriously. She was an Ethiopian immigrant from a culture that practices female genital mutilation. She didn't appreciate my suggesting that it sounded like the counterpart of circumcision for boys, and what was the big deal about it. Glaring at me, she replied something like, "Not quite. It's a totally savage custom invented and perpetuated to safeguard male 'property rights' and their egos by destroying the woman's sex drive and self-confidence. Wives endorse the practice in order to safeguard marriage bonds. Male circumcision is merely a permanent reminder to young boys of their vulnerability, a special admonition to keep their imminent testosterone from inspiring a challenge to the incumbent leadership. The only similarity is that both indignities are disguised as a beneficial, sanctified honor to the victim."

It sounds like the ritual didn't have the intended effect on her. What became of her?

We kept in touch. In graduate school her thesis was a study of the ways that parents collude with society to "shape" their children. We had lots of spirited arguments. She saw much of our behavior and societal structures in evolutionary terms, arguing that "male-female partnering, the minimal family, so to speak, probably started as gang-rape protection for the female and property ownership protection for the male. Corresponding protection and nurturing of offspring resulted in lower infant mortality rates, hence more numerous and healthier, longer-living warriors. Warriors prevailed who could spend more time and energy perfecting their craft while other family members gathered the food, hunted, or stood guard,—all of which inadvertently instilled and perpetuated the family structure. The neighborhood families benefited accordingly with more well-trained, healthy, hardy warriors.

Over time, the families evolved into tribes, organizations for producing food and other goods together with serving the need for security and succession, health care, education, and general welfare. Then, as tribes agglomerated into communities and ultimately into nation states, the more successful ones formed organizations, each one functionally specialized to augment or replace those functions previously conducted largely within the family or tribal unit. I recall her speculating that the nuclear family, like a man's nipples or tailbone, might be just an obsolete vestige of evolution.

That perspective leads directly to the macro-family construct, which I've been almost ready to discuss with you. I wish she was in our chat-room with us.

Me too, but for your information, I also had some inputs that she at least found to be illuminating.

Oh good grief. I keep forgetting about the male ego here. Please tell me, Mr. Wonderful, of your illuminating insights ... sorry! I've been more than a little preoccupied and at moments our communication gets muddied with other agendas, and I shouldn't let that happen. My apologies.

Accepted. And I'll bet you're not going to enlighten me about your preoccupation—maybe a relationship at home you are missing more than you want to?

Something like that, but it's a bit closer than home. What else did your chemistry lab partner have to say about evolving family structures?

Let's see. She claimed that in America during the last century, government largely replaced the nuclear family in taking responsibility for welfare, notably, if imperfectly, health care, food, and minimal housing. With less consistency, welfare elements for the middle class have been incorporated as well, supporting—she would say "intervening in", community relations and education, job markets and industrial relations, security, and safety. Although government maintains responsibility and regulatory control, it utilizes specialized private sector entities to provide the necessary programs, products, and services. She contended that as a result, we are saddled with archaic, functionally specialized institutions in both private and public sectors, inevitable in any resource-scarce, conflict-ridden society.

Aha, the other half of the macro-family imperative! And why "archaic?"

She argued that evolution didn't provide for subsequent population and technology explosions, resulting in proliferation of weapons and decline of essential jobs, ecology overload, family disintegration, ethnic animosities, the sudden availability of mindless and destabilizing mass media information, rich-poor distancing, specialization, and power concentration of producers in influencing government.

That's very close to what I've been observing. More of you Earthlings must begin to recognize that resources are no longer scarce, just poorly distributed, and that conflict costs are no longer paid exclusively by the vanquished. With more widespread enlightenment, you will see increasing pressures on organizations to broaden their mandates. It's already started:

- *Voters want more than governance and security from government. They want health, education, welfare, even expressions of recognition and approval.*

- *Government agencies want more regulatory control; as well as recognition, support, and affection from constituents. They want to choose and conduct the research, development, and programs in their areas. And, of course, each agency wants the overarching responsibility for multi-agency missions: national security, intelligence, economic development, etc.*

- *Non-profits want permission to engage in profit-making initiatives.*

- *Students want career certifications and networking, status, and recreation. Most are adept at minimizing any intrusive exposure to actual education.*

- *Protestors want social responsibility, community development, and compassionate employment from companies. Profit for shareholders is considered sinful.*

- *As your consumers and voters chose their products, services, and leaders, they also seem to need approbation and affiliation. This need often distorts their acquisition decision as well as how the products, services, and leaders are marketed.*

Did your planet go through a similar scenario?

Almost identical challenges faced us with the result that our more powerful and enlightened tribes assumed production and self-governance functions as our producers acquired more socially responsible roles. The resulting "macro-families" were basically the same whether they evolved from tribes or production enterprises—some were even of hybrid origin. Surprisingly, their interaction with government was far healthier than their antecedents' had been.

So if you don't self-destruct soon, you just might gradually move toward the macro-family structuring which we find so successful at home, sort of tribes with brains and enterprises with hearts. Maybe this planet needs to have some of its large, specialized organizations become less specialized in mission and mandate; virtually replicating in large scale, the synergistic, and multiple functions of the traditional family. Sort of what might be called macro-families.

Can you explain your macro-family phenomena to me a bit further?

I'll try. Earth's traditional nuclear family is rapidly declining as society's basic building block. On the other hand, there is a growing trend of traditionally specialized entities, such as companies, government and non-government agencies, and educational and philanthropic institutions, each seeking to broaden their mandates in order to encompass more functions. This tendency demonstrates society's need and readiness for the macro-family.

Functional specialization made sense when scarcity of resources and technologies were the dominant organizational imperatives, but as societal needs of a global population expand, the corresponding needs and opportunities for organizations with broader, more diverse, and synergistic mandates become manifest. This can be visualized as, say the producer of goods and services also providing health, education, welfare, spiritual, and civic services to its constituents, or a philanthropic charity incorporating "profitable" production of goods and services.

Today, your specialized entities go as far as regulators permit and are nonetheless vilified as mandate poachers or tax-evaders. The Israeli kibbutz, the Amish village, diasporas comprised of recent immigrants from closely networked cultures; some of these exemplify Earthlings' potential receptivity to the macro-family idea.

Finally, the macro-family concept should not be viewed as a threat to your civilization. Rather, it should be legalized, developed, and encouraged as supportive to both the state and to the nuclear family, just as we do at home.

Interestingly, your observations match the precepts that underlie solid engineering design and analysis. If the external challenges change along with characteristics of the internal system components, we'll often change the subsystem configurations and tasks allocated to the subsystems.

So make it happen! Just remember that everything makes sense. Surprises happen because people weren't paying attention or looking at the right things or reasoning from the right conceptual models. Mysteries are no longer mysterious once you learn what you didn't know when things seemed mysterious.

A final admonition: Your mantra, "The truth shall set you free," only works if accompanied by compatible culture, institutions, and change agents with power and implementation mechanisms. Otherwise the truth may just set you aside or in concrete. Reality is your friend, so accept and work with it.

Got it. And my reality right now is telling me to take a break. What with all the sensory and cerebral input, I'm in overload—and it's not all that bad! ☺ Tomorrow, at the regular time?

Of course.

SESSION 31

I admit the "macro-family" concept is new to me, but not the basic concept of optimizing a system's design configuration. Doing so, in my experience, is always challenged by implementation barriers. Do you see any major obstacle in our moving forward with the macro-family implementation?

Yes, several challenges. Stakeholders with power and authority must relinquish some of both and be quite astute about it. Certain cherished beliefs and cultural characteristics will be challenged.

Such as?

Integrity may be a major challenge. Integrity is so pervasive on our home planet; I'd never given it a thought, until looking at a place that doesn't have much of it. A major challenge is moving away from your culture's widespread reliance on short-term expediency over integrity, persuading Earthlings to recognize integrity's far-reaching benefit and cost.

What do you mean? We Earthlings are honest and truth-telling almost always.

Our style of integrity is a bit broader than yours. It's consistency as to what one says, does, and is; that's what makes it powerful. It

confers economy of organization and communication; hence effi-
ciency of resources utilization, enrichment of relationships, and
resiliency of community.

Once you think about it, it's sort of obvious—why isn't there
more of it here? Maybe integrity is a luxury, a trait that doesn't
evolve readily when the primary challenge is survival. But what if
survival becomes dependant upon collaboration or what if survival
is no longer the most important issue? Perhaps as technology replaces
scarcity with affluence and civilization evolves, integrity may
become an affordable luxury or even a necessity for long-term sur-
vival on your planet, too.

In the interest of honesty and truth-telling, I'm feeling a bit
insulted and misunderstood. I believe we value and practice
integrity and you're not reading us accurately. And let's not forget how you only gradually revealed yourself to me. Wasn't that
a bit of deception on your part, calling for an integrity hiatus?

Chauvinistic self-deception on your part is not the same as—is
that what you Earthlings call a "red herring?" Are you teasing me? I
can't tell without visual contact. I wish there was some way we
could be together without "being together". In any case, you may be
right, and I didn't mean to insult you.

But I'm convinced the topic is important. Here, take a look at
my notes I'll email.

NOTES: Earthlings much of the time espouse one thing, but do
another. The consequences appear monumental and frightening.
For example:

- *The sanctity of life is preached everywhere, but ethnic and reli-*
  gious genocide, mass starvation, public health disasters, and
  domestic violence are ongoing. Each occurrence is perceived as

*unique and is vigorously condemned, although not always imme-
diately. Remedial action is taken only under narrow conditions.*

- *Everyone claims to be opposed to the illegal drugs industry. Yet it
  flourishes at immense cost to the planet, financially as well as in
  terms of human suffering, corruption, and overload of government regulation and law enforcement. Knowledgeable advocates
  of the "war on drugs" must understand the limited utility of their
  initiatives to control sources or impose various law enforcement
  initiatives to control distribution. They must also know that
  workable alternatives exist, which include decriminalization
  and medical treatment. Yet their advocacy persists, placing
  self-justification and punishment of "offenders" ahead of genuine
  problem solving, even ahead of their own financial self-interests.
  Strange.*

- *Parents raise their children with "good intentions," but often
  with disingenuous techniques of child rearing. Parents often
  exercise control via lies, conditional love, and approval. This
  makes parenting easier and ostensibly prepares children for survival in even more hostile environments. But the residue of mis-
  trusting relationships and self-doubts—how can these children
  successfully interrelate in marriage, family, work, and society in
  adulthood?*

- *Antics of political candidates are both amusing and frightening.
  Challengers demonize and denigrate incumbents, stimulate fears
  and desires among constituents, and over-promise what they will
  do if elected. Incumbents claim credit for their predecessors'
  accomplishments, and condemn the inexperience and unpredict-
  ability of their challengers. Since issue-oriented voters seldom
  change their minds, candidates concentrate on the apathetic or*

indecisive electorate, barraging them with emotionally charged "wedge-issues."

• *In addition, the absence of integrity as a primary societal value has fostered a cumbersome, ad hoc monetary and economic system. The treatment and protection of capital—the surrogate for anything considered valuable, takes on enormous importance when not backed by societal and interpersonal integrity. Tremendous effort and attention must be devoted to accumulating, safeguarding, stealing, borrowing, analyzing, trading, and taxing capital assets. The complexity which the absence of integrity requires complicates and disguises economic realities from the public, and even confuses the economic policy wonks and scholars. For example, they pontificate that capital will "create" jobs if diverted to the right uses—can you imagine? If capital creates jobs, I asked one of them, how many jobs are created by file cabinets? There's a difference between job creators and resource enablers. He just looked at me as if I was from another planet. Hah! I almost told him.*

These misconceptions and complexities help maintain damaging aberrations in allocation and utilization of resources, in management of risks, and in crisis responses—all of which would be greatly simplified and improved if the people, their culture and institutions properly reflected the value of integrity. Such contradictions can't persist in a civilization that prizes integrity—and should no longer be tolerated, considering this planet's increasingly ominous future.

The consequent pressures on leadership will ultimately prove inexorable but essential:

- *Union leaders will have to tell their membership that the global labor force is soon to be ten times larger than what's needed to do what's needed.*

- *Government leaders or candidates will have to acknowledge that income redistribution by means of employment salaries, if limited to necessary jobs, won't work. They'll have to rely on unnecessary jobs or just give the money away—a kind of "welfare" if viewed traditionally.*

- *Company executives will have to tell investors that since the Internet increasingly discloses where true costs and added value reside in both production and after-sale use of products and services, that these disclosures will impact pricing pressures, hence earnings and return on investment.*

- *The military will have to report to constituents that if disproportionate response to threats, including torture, death squads, civilian casualties, and massive infrastructure damage are out, and the killing or capture of warriors is out, we're not going to get much TV coverage; hence, no budget increases, and hence, declared victories.*

- *Advocates and protectors of various claimed "rights" may be forced to limit rhetoric and constituents' aspirations to accommodate to the emerging constraints of environmental degradation, counter-terrorism, and population pressures.*

END OF NOTES

Hmm, since our leaders are not about to say and do these things, does it follow that our leaders are intrinsically resistant to integrity? If so, what can we do about it? Maybe we can pick this up tomorrow, same time?

Good comment. Yes, tomorrow.

Session 32

You posed the interesting question of whether your leaders are intrinsically resistant to integrity. From my brief observation I'd say leaders will exercise integrity if, for no other reason than that all things being equal, their constituents will eventually demand it. We all prefer integrity in ourselves and others, as long as our immediate pleasure/pain considerations don't dominate.

I suppose that's right. I just bought a flat-screen television from a salesman whose demeanor and dishonest sales pitch demonstrated his lack of integrity. But the price was the lowest I'd found. So even forewarned, I decided to take my chances with his promises of after-sales service. What might have induced me to prize integrity more and go elsewhere?

Maybe nothing, when you consider the local, short-term tradeoffs. But here's a larger, long-term example of what happened on my planet. You've talked considerably about the loose-canon freelance terrorist problem. The various barriers you site seem to come down to the absence of a unified, global strategy and program. Under similar circumstances, we established an enforceable agreement among the nation states. That collaboration happened because the governments were afraid for it not to. It also required a level of sacrifice and endorsement from each country's citizens, which required new levels of—and enforcement mechanisms for, mutual trust and communication between government and citizens in that anti-terrorist area. Nobody liked the loss of privacy and freedom of action, but it was obviously the only way to contain the threats.

Interesting. Then what happened?

Gradually, other global issues resulted in a group of enforceable agreements in WMD, pandemics, corruption, environment, and trade. Slowly but surely, integrity took hold, both in international relations and domestically. The value of one's "word," consistency of character, and establishment of mutual trust became vital in dealing quickly and effectively with extra-agreement events. This word-character-trust, so costly to establish, took on synergistic value of its own and became embedded in the culture. All this just happened as the result of long-term pragmatism and growing awareness of the danger to survival.

Well, we're very pragmatic and resourceful, as you have observed. We're handling these things on a case-by-case basis, government-to-government, and it works for us, too.

But as I look ahead, you don't have time, and as I look back, you don't have the history. Do you honestly think you'll survive, continuing to deal with these threats by ad hoc, individual, country-to-country deals? Get serious. Two-party negotiation seems to work on this planet if one of the negotiators clearly dominates, or if there is a third arbitrator with power to run the negotiation process or if both the negotiators see resolution more advantageous than not. With your planet's history of conflict resolution, I'm not encouraged.

You're saying that either a single country government, or a combination of several, must take over control of all the others by force or enlightened self-interest and then that monolithic—how could that possibly happen?

I'd guess that the only way you'll get enlightened self-interest is if a preponderance of your privileged, networked, powerful people simultaneously see a carrot or stick propelling them to relinquish some control and relative affluence for a new pleasure or pain-avoidance.

I think we need to think of some other possibilities. Our recent moves toward world government have consistently failed, including the League of Nations and United Nations. It simply doesn't work on this planet.

Not so fast. As I read your history, those were not explicit, purposeful moves toward world government, but rather loose alliances of victorious gladiators hiding their retribution programs with a mask of altruism. It's as if Earthlings are embarrassed at winning a war, so they try to ennoble it retroactively with some gesture toward global harmony, but without committing serious resources or relinquishing any prerogatives. Now you're in a very different situation; one in which survival of the planet, or at least large chunks of your "civilization," are at risk, thanks to globalization.

Well, maybe.

Think of these past attempts as "world government light" or a federation for which you have several viable examples.

But why should that make the defining difference? Is that what happened on your planet?

When the traditional sociopolitical structures encountered globalization, we encountered major turmoil, which made the public frightened, and therefore pliable. Fortunately, we had a network of think-tanks and universities that joined intellect, understanding, and resources with the also-frightened and pliable elite. We didn't declare world government, but studies and simulations demon-

*strated the absolute need for global integration of systems for insur-
ing international security: intelligence, counterterrorism, arms
control, energy, environmental protection, trading networks, public
health monitoring, and communications regulation. It was obvious
that all of these things had to be overseen by one controlling entity.
Committees of local governments could monitor and improve these
threats to the planet, but not manage them. Of course, we still have
regional and local governments with maximum autonomy in all
areas that are not planet-threatening.*

Is that where you see Earth heading?

*Either that, or to oblivion. But things are not as grim as I'd orig-
inally thought. Don't forget that we selected this planet because it
looked hopelessly on the verge of imploding, simply because of ludicrous mismanagement. Now I've come to see my initial forecast as
overly pessimistic. Earth just might be different.*

Tell me more. And, please, tell me what you're really thinking.

*The deeper I look, I find a subtle but unique resiliency here. I
believe there is a set of conditions on Earth that could assure stability and effectively handle whatever challenges emerge. I grant you
that the imminent challenges are so formidable that to attain that
set of conditions soon enough seems questionable. In order to transition to a permanently stable world like ours, you must overcome
strongly entrenched anachronistic traits. These traits were first
shaped by survivability, then by geography, and finally by modes of
competition, conflict, and consolidation. Currently, competitive
marketing is so pervasive and effective that it subordinates survival
instincts, values of intellect, and creativity in favor of narcissistic,
mindless consumption.*

So what are these conditions for survival and stability?

First and foremost there are some crucial values; values which must be held with reverence and conviction:

- The sanctity of life and its perpetuation;

- Adequate security, health, and nourishment; and

- Necessary sociopolitical infrastructures and their institutional channels and motivators.

These are sufficient for an autocracy whose citizens are controllable and whose behavior doesn't require much sophistication. But with unconstrained access to information, to WMD, to international travel, and with population growth that is saturating ecologies, the challenges call for enlightened, flexible, creative behavior by the populace. This can only happen with growth and development of the individual and the state in a balanced symbiosis, ruling out autocracy as a stable mode. Thus, democracy becomes the only viable alternative, a democracy whose people are educated, actualized, and participatory.

This in turn creates additional needs:

- Integrity and transparency; honesty in communication and within oneself. Reverence for privacy can become less important if integrity and transparency become revered.

- Education sufficient for intelligently grasping concepts, and understanding issues and situations; at least sufficiently to choose, monitor, and evaluate leaders and representatives.

- Emotional and intellectual maturity, which are essential for understanding and accepting reality. Only then can there be dispassionate assessment of situations, formulation of sensible strate-

gic plans with understanding of risk tradeoffs, and effective management of change implementation.

- *Justice and fairness in law enforcement, sociopolitical, and economic endeavors.*

- *Institutional development assistance, ongoing surveillance and assessment of institutional performance, vulnerabilities, and opportunities for further adaptation and growth.*

Not intrinsically essential, but good indicators of such a society, include:

- *Conflict and tension, its understanding, acceptance, and/or resolution, recognizing that conflict and tension are ubiquitous: in the structure of molecules, in procreation of survivable species, in education and human development.*

- *Humility, indicative of receptivity to new situations and alternatives.*

- *Humor for flexibility, balance, and acceptance of the incongruous and where it might lead.*

- *Reverence and vigilance; life as a temporary, anomalous gift, which calls for vigilance and celebration.*

- *Tolerance; perception of "others" as less human is inconsistent with equality and justice.*

- *Aesthetics, a natural gateway and enticement to the abstract; vital, yet ineffable.*

With all due respect, that's an awful lot of detail to assimilate, let alone effectuate.

Of course it is, and I've come to realize that your swashbuckling, reactive quarterback-like executives and their "coaches" don't like checklists and criteria. Such mind-numbing details can deflect concentration that is vital for immediate crisis-stomping and PR events. However, while cheerfully and confidently moving ahead, it's useful to have a viable destination in mind, especially if there are forks in the road, few of which lead to survival.

I never expected to be emotionally involved with someone sounding more like a Greek chorus than me. Are you always this grim?

I think you know that I'm not, and it's not the company; it's your messed-up planet! Let me end this on a positive note: The tedious listings above? They all interconnect, and some are located in semi-stable positions. It takes very little to start an avalanche; just having the right conditions and finding the trigger-points—it's easier to do if you've first mapped the avalanches. So, for example, if you could magically break the integrity-transparency bottlenecks, most of the many elements I just listed would get fixed or improved.

That's encouraging. Same time tomorrow?

With pleasure.

SESSION 33

Tell me honestly. Are you really a musicologist?

Yes, of course. I'm also a composer. That goes with the territory. Why do you ask?

Well, looking over yesterday's session, which was so well-organized and comprehensive; it has me wondering if you're not really a systems engineer. If not, you certainly could have been.

I get it. You probably think that composers pick a few notes at random, designate them as a melody, and then just compile a string of variations until the length is about right. Haven't you ever noticed the exquisitely systematic structure underlying some of Bach's ... never mind. So what does a well-organized systems engineer do at this point?

Hey, I was just complimenting you on ... OK, I'd devise a systems framework that would accommodate the elements you listed yesterday, and more. As you say, I'm just a grubby systems engineer, so I naturally think of the world as a system with powerful—and powerless, stakeholders. But then, upon closer examination, I see this global system as a hierarchy of intercon-

215

nected systems: global, regional, national, municipal, family, relationship, self. Each of these systems has a set of stakeholders, which can be detailed according to their intrinsic attributes: roles and goals, resources and recourses, internal strengths and weaknesses, external threats and opportunities, intentions and initiatives, and consensus and commitment. Each of the systems' attributes can be detailed structurally or functionally with generic attributes designated in economic, sociological, political, behavioral, or cultural terms—whatever is appropriate to our purpose. This just restates the process I've been chattering about all along.

Yes, I recognize it. And I never said you were grubby; you're not. So how do I grapple with all the above detail?

Thank you. If we had three-dimensional paper, we could construct an XYZ chart utilizing the three "dimensions" underlined above: hierarchy of systems, their attributes, and stakeholders. But we don't have such paper so it's easier to devise a spreadsheet that accommodates these dimensions and their details.

Yes. Since I didn't think to bring any of our multi-dimensional paper on this trip, I'll try your spreadsheet exercise and get right back to you.

Fine. My only suggestion is to make this first attempt no more detailed or complete than necessary, because you'll find you want to change column headings and/or levels of detail as you get into it.

I'm back, and that last bit of advice was useful. In working with my spreadsheet, I found it helpful to designate these four groupings of stakeholders, respectively endowed with and guardians of:

- *Resources*

- *Authority*

- *Culture*

- *Knowledge*

Our previous analyses and my roaming around, confirm that there is dissonance among these stakeholders at all levels, global to individual, in part owing to external turmoil's reverberating to each of the four stakeholder groups as well.

- **Resources**, *particularly the supply and demand of oil and labor are out of balance.*

- **Authority** *is chaotic because systems of governance evolved during a relatively stable era no longer work given the advent of gangs, warlords, and autonomous terrorist cells.*

- **Cultures** *and their sustaining institutions have lost relevance and influence with the profligate availability of weapons and drugs, sex, and telecommunication.*

- **Knowledge** *of WMD is proliferating, making enforceable treaties vital. Knowledge stakeholders could offer solutions, but are seldom trusted.*

Ouch! Much of this we've discussed empirically. Now, I'm gratified to see it emerge from your more structured analyses, but ouch!

Yes. In essence I've recast what I see as this planet's situation; in particular, that it is in the first stages of what at home we've called the "Enlightenment Revolution." It's especially chaotic here because your various technologies have advanced faster than the existing leadership and traditional institutions can digest. The consequences are uncontrolled proliferation of weapons, drugs, information, and indignation. How would you as a systems engineer proceed from here?

How would I proceed? First, I'd stock up on tequila and limes, a bathing suit, and Viagra, and update my passport and investment portfolio. Then I'd go searching for gorgeous extra-terrestrial women, preferably on South Sea or Caribbean islands. Or if you would just come with me, I'd only need the passport.

Please be serious.

I almost am. OK, I'd first research the next level of detail in the Enlightenment Revolution you've sketched, try to discover the key stakeholders, their hot buttons, avalanche triggers, and bottlenecks. I'd deliberately do that in an unstructured way.

Isn't that sort of what we've been doing?

Yes, I guess so. But then I'd sketch the system's structure, an anatomy chart from which I could *systematically* produce a framework or spreadsheet, which would allow me to tabulate the salient problems and potential remedies. Next, I'd even try to rate or rank their priority according to a few formal criteria. I wouldn't go into too much detail or mathematical sophistication, at least not on this first pass. That's due to my limited data and expertise, credentials, and the limited attention span of anyone with power to implement what I'd discover and then advocate. It would also help to avoid getting locked into a viewpoint prematurely.

That sounds productive. What would your spreadsheet look like?

I don't have a clue but let me work on it and I'll report back. Meanwhile, talk to me. How are you? What have you been doing?

I've been out and about, not talking with Earthlings at all; just watching, listening, thinking, staring at the sky, and wondering if I'm homesick right now and if I'll be "Earth-sick" when I return home. That's all—except that I can sense lots of turmoil and agitation in the non-cognitive zone of my consciousness. And you are constantly in my conscious thoughts. Very strange—and yourself?

I'm OK. Thanks for telling me and I'll respond, but first things first. I've tried several configurations. The one that seems to work best for me is based on the human as my basic system component or building block. But my human at various times functions in at least eight different roles: Buyer and Voter, Worker and Player, Fighter and Advocate, Procreator and Nurturer. Each of the eight functions is conducted in its correspondingly distinct setting and each setting is part of its specialized institutions. Here is the brief chart that I came up with:

FUNCTIONS	SETTINGS	INSTITUTIONS
Buyer	Point of sale	Marketplace
Voter	Voting precinct	Political system
Worker	Workplace	Private/Public sector
Player	Recreation	Recreation facility
Fighter	Battlefield	Combat Organization
Advocate	Town hall	Legal system
Procreator	Relationship	Family/Community
Nurturer	Health/School	State

I could diagram all this with boxes and arrows, which sometimes can be especially helpful in depicting cross connections, or their absence. However, with all those arrows, it might begin to resemble Custer's Last Stand.

Well yes, and we really want to identify and prioritize problems and remedies associated with a function, setting, institution, and/or combinations or components of them. My observations confirm that the preponderance of problems and remedies relate directly to those pesky stakeholders, or the attributes—resources, authority, culture and knowledge—they respectively inject adequately or inadequately.

Exactly. So this suggests three spreadsheets, one each for Functions, Settings, and Institutions. Take SETTINGS for example. Rows of its spreadsheet would be labeled Point of Sale, Voting Precinct, Workplace, or whatever, with columns labeled RESOURCES, AUTHORITY, CULTURE, and KNOWLEDGE.

I'm not sure I can stand much more of this excitement. ☺

SETTINGS	RESOURCES	AUTHORITY	CULTURE	KNOWLEDGE	TOTAL SCORE
Point of Sale					
Voting Precinct					
Workplace					
Recreation					
Battlefield					
Town Hall					
Relationship					
Health					

Kid around all you like, but this can be powerful stuff. Any individual cell provides space for rating its row-column combination, for example workplace/resources. The rating might be simply a judgment of good/bad, or the numerical total of scored multiple criteria; criteria such as "appropriate," "adequate,", or "adaptable." The right-hand column is reserved for such totals.

My, my, you are systematic! Seriously, I'm impressed to see how this sort of framework allows, even encourages working at an otherwise obnoxious level of detail.

Incidentally, depending on your purpose, rather than stakeholder attributes, such a spreadsheet might be used to rate the stakeholders themselves. And of course the rows and columns could be disaggregated into sub rows and sub columns. You can make these constructs as detailed and complicated or rudimentary as you wish, depending on your purpose. All of which is to remind you that we're illustrating tools, not rules.

How poetic! Well, I'm impressed, but I have to ask: is all this kind of work involved, in your experience, worthwhile?

Yes, in three ways. Working at this level of detail produces a rating mosaic that really does provide a prioritized identification of problem-solution-opportunities, confirming my ideas or redirecting me to the priority areas for attention which are frequently a surprise. This level of detail also reveals broader insights; the spreadsheet might reveal that the products and services are right, but the providers are toxic to the progress of civilization—religion might be a good example, or fossil fuels as another. Finally, as I work away at my spreadsheet, an inner-voice may intervene, conveying the sense that I'm working in the wrong domain, validating an irrelevant hypothesis, or needing more in-depth information. I find invaluable, sometimes disconcerting, insights indirectly emerging in conducting this methodical process.

And it must keep you off the streets and out of bars at night. I like that. ☺

It's been known to do just that.

So now it's my turn to put in some work on all this. Spreadsheets here I come!

You know where to find me. ☺

SESSION 34

I haven't heard from you. Is everything OK?

I've been busily immersed in spreadsheets. It's not Monday Night Football, but ... actually from detailed spreadsheets, as you'd suggested, I was able to tabulate and rate a long list of challenges and responses.

Excellent. That's just what I would have done. What are your results?

It's still a bit crude, but in summary, the primary challenges are, well, challenging:

- *WMD; perpetrators ranging from nations to Non-Governmental Organizations to cells or individuals;*

- *Energy and Environment;*

- *Economic Stability and Income distribution;*

- *Health and Welfare;*

- *Employment and Education;*

- *Conflict Management; and*

- *Development of the individual, family, and community.*

Good lord! Sorry I asked.

Please don't despair. Even without invoking your deity, it's actually not quite as formidable as it seems. My onerously detailed spreadsheet highlights a multitude of problem areas. But there are a few initiatives, each of which would ameliorate several of these areas.

What initiatives?

Here's a preliminary sort of "wish list," which is not complete, but illustrative of initiatives which I, and your systems spreadsheet, would advocate:

- *Mobilize and redirect some of your S&T; convert the culprit into savior.*

- *Establish universal conscription; a draft where each young person and each new retiree devotes a year or two to public service. In exchange, draftees receive post-service benefits: educational, medical, housing, and entrepreneurial or job-placement assistance.*

- *Modernize and accelerate education and human development; content, institutions, and processes.*

- *Do everything possible to move toward limited global federation. The planet's survival requires it.*

- *Reconstitute your welfare programs to actually promote welfare. Properly instituted, they will protect and enhance, and thereby provide well-being for the rich and poor.*

- *Fix your global energy and environmental problems.*

- *Motivate the media to clarify and promote reality over fantasy and the joys of giving over consuming.*

- *Use <u>proactive</u> reporting to fight your most egregious frauds: illegal commerce in drugs, sex, weapons, and corruption in both the private and public sectors. Transparency isn't enough; in fact it's often a deceptive euphemism.*

As your collaborator, I'm totally impressed. As an Earthling, I'm totally intimidated. Your list is a very tall order! It seems like a multitude of interconnected strategies and programs. How in the world could we start it, let alone make any of it happen in a timely, effective manner?

A crucial question, of course. I don't have the definitive answer for Earth in this critical period. I can tell you that on my planet, either by design, desperation, or luck, we devised a partnership of our intellectuals. This group figured out what was needed, in collaboration with our producer-sector people, who knew how to mobilize and use resources in major programs. This proved to be the key to our vital development.

It led to solving energy and environment problems, largely via development of nuclear and solar energy; solving food and health problems, via genetic engineering, plus pragmatic pandemic and demographic prevention policies. A restive populace was pacified by instituting enlightened, proactive programs, which assured basic welfare and human and civil rights in exchange for law-abiding behavior of citizens and their communities. You'll recognize these problems as the key ones your planet is confronting, which if resolved could unblock the economic and sociopolitical advances that seem unattainable right now.

What you just said is indeed crucial! You've restored my hope that with enlightened direction, the advantages your planet now enjoys could come to us as well.

Exactly. First the intellectuals analyzed and designed the changes required. Then they and the private sector implemented them, including the important contribution of upgrading leadership in government and private organizations. An unanticipated assist came from the illegal drug industry, recognizing that a less-chaotic global governance and economy would be to their advantage, at least in the short-term.

Governments followed with audit, jurisprudence, and transparency initiatives. The few journalists who understood what was happening worked with private sector media specialists to force-feed enlightenment into otherwise entertainment-focused, semi medicated publics.

It still sounds very complicated. Could we do anything like that?

Well, our private sector executives seem to have had a broader education and understanding of how interests of organizations and stakeholders depended on the long-term global situation. Also, we had major environmental and terrorism incidents which had a reality focusing effect—you're not quite there yet. Our people were very willing, even enthusiastic, about relinquishing some privacy for unobtrusive surveillance and control. Non-lethal weapons and fences, cerebral chip transponders for remote interrogation, enlightened justice and rehabilitation systems ... these facilitated our major transition from paralyzing fear and chaos.

I believe that explains how our "metamorphosis" occurred. I hope yours can succeed too, perhaps with less death and destruction than ours. What do you think?

What I think is that I need to think about all this, maybe overnight. Is that OK with you?

Absolutely. Same time tomorrow.

SESSION 35

Some of your wish-list items look improbable without gifted leadership. Have you thought about that aspect at all?

I have, and I agree. Gifted leadership is necessary, even if not sufficient. America's governmental leadership did not retain its edge during the recent decades when there were no serious external enemies. A prosperous economy and industry, technologies, and socioeconomic institutions made leadership and its continuing development almost unnecessary in government. Your most talented leaders were drawn to the more challenging and lucrative private sector.

Your election process, with various affluent special interests and apathetic and uninformed voters, produces candidates and winners who, if not initially venal and mindless, soon learn to behave that way. Would-be leaders who are intelligent and truthful don't get into office, or stay there for very long if they do. The bright ones who try to "dumb down" to accommodate, unless adept at deception, don't project sincerity. If they radiate true integrity, that just makes the hedonistic voters feel guilty and antagonistic.

I don't disagree with what you're saying, but we've done rather well despite these flaws. Don't you think?

Amazingly so, but now the leadership challenge is much greater. Leaders must project integrity to maintain the loyalty of constituents and hopefully win over third-party bystanders as well as elements of their opponents' supporters. They must also be competent in dealing with conflicts, because modern weapons and telecommunication make the stakes so much higher. A less-obvious aspect of terrorism is its negative impact on the integrity of people. At its most basic, integrity can never flourish without terror-free, fair, decisive conflict resolution. People are too angry, skeptical, or frightened for it to work otherwise.

So it looks like major changes are imminent and maybe cataclysmic. Anyone can access weapons, Internet collaborations, and initiatives financed by drugs or ransom. In such an environment, leadership counts!

Your portrayal makes things look almost hopeless. Is that how you see things here?

Not at all. It's a mixed situation. Here, I'll e-mail you some of my recent ruminations.

NOTES: Rational self-interest may not be enough to save this planet. My major concern is timing. Consider how long it takes Earthlings to stop smoking or to come to grips with global warming, AIDS, or political misconduct. Their creativity in procrastination is awesome. All the tricks for evading short-term discomfort while ignoring the potential for long-term benefit are well-known and widely used. Nevertheless, I am far more optimistic now than I was earlier, for several reasons:

- *There is an obvious urgency for overt steps to save this planet. The need will be apparent to wider audiences soon. For the first* time, the <u>*impoverished and the affluent will find common cause*</u> *in fearing ecology disasters, rampant disease, and armed, lawless despots.*

- *Earthlings' previous technology revolutions impacted supplier-consumer products and services. The information revolution is distinct in providing lateral networking also. It permits each consumer—the recipient of information, to instantly become a supplier as well, with products and services all easily affordable and accessible. The implications for <u>rapid, potent societal reconfiguration and action</u> are just beginning to be recognized.*

- <u>*Advanced technology*</u> *in sensors, predictive models, data analysis tools, and information dissemination will add great sophistication to surveillance, distribution and interpretation of what has happened, is happening, and may happen, all with accuracy and timeliness for remedial action in support of planet-saving work.*

- *There is an economic push-pull that might be fortuitous. The demise of <u>work as the income redistribution mechanism</u> traditionally linking the middle class to upper and lower economic classes presents a major challenge. The answer presents another challenge, the imperative for <u>responsible, informed, educated, emotionally mature citizens</u>, which is only achievable by lots of humanistic work! This calls for a simultaneous transition in cultural values, sociopolitical institutions, and the economy, as well as work-force skills—very challenging but doable!*

America's states and many smaller countries were delineated according to land resources, populations, and politics more than two centuries ago. Now with telecommunication, modern transporta-

tion, and the migration of critical issues and opportunities to national, regional, and local levels, America's state governments and these small countries are simply hotbeds of graft and corruption. You have cities like New York with populations so tightly clustered that only bicycles and fatalistic cab drivers can move within it. Population centers to the north and south consume exorbitant quantities of energy for heating and air-conditioning. There are similar excesses in the industrial sectors as well. The consequent waste in resources, human productivity, and the sociopolitical strains from these anachronistic structures and resource allocations; that waste is enormous. Minor reallocation of these resources could have major impact in addressing some of the issues we've identified.

Observing these archaic organizations from home left us incredulous and amused. Now I see these white elephants and sacred cows very differently. They are almost criminal in wasting resources and harboring graft and corruption, which conceals and constrains vital problem solutions for entire populations. Technologies might create options in sociopolitical and economic dimensions that, once applied, will free resources of all kinds for less ludicrous infrastructure. END OF NOTES.

Wow! What's happened to you? You're not the detached, cynical extraterrestrial I met and have fallen in love with. Anything else?

Yes. Please don't—that's just the kind of comment that, we don't say things like that at home. "Anything else?" you asked. Yes, some of your recently matured technologies could make substantial differences in terms of socioeconomic and cultural advances without inordinate financial or political barriers. I'll mention a few, but there are many more such opportunities:

- *Providing truthful, specific information for consumers, whether they are buying, voting, or learning. Information technologies are no longer the bottleneck, but the content is often contaminated by ignorance or bias at the source. There are many ways to validate information that are not utilized, not because of technology issues, but because of special interests and consumers' ignorance of the value versus cost entailed.*

- *Offering mate selection optimizers at controllable levels of intrusiveness. It's easy to do, and vital to protect society and minimize destructive, painful interpersonal experiences.*

- *Supplying modern health care and education systems. Protecting the existing processes and establishments currently prevails over enlightened use of proven procedures and their technologies. Bureaucratic arthritis, reverence for white elephants, and excessive indirect costs create enormous unnecessary expenses.*

Further, there are applications on my planet which you could emulate with relatively modest <u>new technologies. A few examples:</u>

- *Smart and flexible mass transportation vehicles and systems;*

- *Single-person backpack propulsion;*

- *Small-scale plants for water desalinization, biomass recycling, and electricity. Currently on Earth, unbelievable quantities of copper, steel, and fossil fuels are devoted to vulnerable and otherwise inefficient delivery of these commodities.*

- *Advanced monitoring and surveillance for protection of the young, ill, elderly, and property; and*

• *Bio-implants and genetic manipulation. Earth scientists must learn how to do this selectively with the kinds of safeguards we've developed.*

When I first started this project, I saw the Earthlings as primitive savages; avaricious, ignorant, self-absorbed, and exceedingly unattractive. But observing and conversing with them, well, somehow I'm beginning to see them almost as "noble savages."

Initially this planet seemed just like some theme park, populated with ludicrous cartoon characters. Civilization on Earth is still just beginning, evolving from a predatory, resource-scarce heredity. What exists here is an almost infinitude of random mutations, a miniscule percentage of which stumbled into host-parasite symbioses long enough to just barely squirt their genes into the next evolutionary success. How durable must be any traits that survived their millions of years' evolution.

You can see how tightly geography has shaped lives on Earth by noting seemingly trivial details. Until the advent of refrigeration, most population growth and productive activity clustered in the temperate zones. The temperate zone in the Northern Hemisphere has substantially more land mass than that of the Southern Hemisphere. This advantageously conferred economies of scale and markets proximity with corresponding benefits in agriculture, economic, and sociopolitical developments. Many Northerners feel culturally, morally, and intellectually superior, ignorant of the comparative advantages geography has provided the Northern Hemisphere.

In the summer, the Northern natives must prepare clothing, shelter, food, and fuel in advance of winter. This geography-enforced discipline is reflected in their community structures, religion, and values. It tends to make some of them dour, joyless, and very aggressive in dealing with taboo-violators, real or imagined. They make

the necessity of deferred or declined gratification into a virtue, taking pride in their lifestyle and values which are actually imposed by a solar system accident. Then perhaps at some level, feeling foolish or envious, they denigrate those who live in more convivial climates. Similarly, coastal residents who trade over great distances and maintain contact with many different cultures feel cosmopolitan and disdainful of those who find what they need locally. For Earthlings to feel superior to other Earthlings seems very important here.
END OF NOTES

I hear you saying that we're so busy grappling with the challenges of geography we remain savages. Where does the "noble" part enter?

Good question. I see your "savage" legacy still evident in your intercommunity relations. But within individual communities that have overcome these challenges, I now see most Earthlings as noble, humane, socially responsible people who genuinely dedicate much of themselves and their resources to helping others and working to develop a responsible, caring society.

After experiencing and understanding deprivation and the merits of building communities, striving for the best possible life on this not-always-benign planet, a sense of mutual dependence has emerged. The development of agriculture and industry, the circumnavigation of the oceans, survival during epidemics and wars, the continuing creation of stable sociopolitical and economic systems ... these all show how courageous, patient, and even heroic the human species is. Somehow, the qualities of sharing, excellence, and independence, which the harsh history fostered, grew—not too shabby!

So where does this leave you?

Since knowing you, I find myself deeply concerned about how this planet might be saved. How would I design a bridge for its survival? The basic components, the building blocks of such a bridge,

234 Managing Global Survival

would have to be the individual Earthling; how he/she behaves and connects to Earth's societal elements and to the continual growth of your civilization.

I'm impressed! Same time tomorrow?

Yes, fine.

SESSION 36

It would help me to hear more about how your planet survived what we're going through.

Of course. I've been somewhat reluctant because of concern that either of us might draw too close a parallel to our history and your future. We need to view our history as analogous but not the template. There's also the risk of getting lost in trivial details. But I'll try.

With some important differences, fundamentally we faced the same challenges. I wish I could say that our far-sighted leadership anticipated and diagnosed the problems and identified the triggers for avalanches to implement the results ultimately achieved.

Not so?

Not so. Our progress, as on planet Earth, evolved with control, including governance largely dominated by what you call the private sector. This pattern of evolution is probably inevitable if only because the prerequisite for success of one state in competition with others must be a strong military. For the military to prevail, whether by conquest or intimidation, it must be backed by a strong economy and loyal citizenry. That in turn calls for a responsive, producer sector and benign government policies. Thus, within prevailing states at least, there is a natural, essential marriage of the military, education, and producer sectors.

I hadn't thought about it but that sounds logical. Of course if any marriage gets too tight or parochial or unbalanced, the household is endangered.

Good point. In any case, what almost happened to us is what's happening here. Proliferation of weapons threatened our military establishments and the dependent populations directly. The governmental and producer sectors' subsequently lost control. Drugs, entertainment, and ubiquitous weapons displaced psychological needs for committed affiliation or loyalty to family or community. Market forces and survival fears spawned proliferations of gangs, militias, and warlords. The general populace, in panic, became increasingly more docile and turned to charismatic leaders who didn't have a clue about how to manage in this new crisis-driven environment.

It sounds terrible and akin to my worst nightmares. What happened next?

Fortunately a few bright executives, understanding the synergies of military, producer, and intellectual establishments had created a combination think-tank and academy. Over the years a network of quiet cells was produced, each incubating enlightened potential leaders, trained via game-simulators and an elite team of scholars. These scholars spanned the fields of history, biology, psychology, sociology, anthropology, philosophy, military science, neuron-psychology, literature, and more; each an expert but capable of working with the other specialists. Collectively they respected rationality, culture, and civilization while focusing on identifying and energizing grass-roots activators of sanity, stability, and progress. It's very hard to generalize from this dynamic, heterogeneous period and as I've told you, I'm no expert.

But surely you can tell me of some lessons learned pertaining to what we should do here.

Let's see if I can mention some "lessons learned" or at least some unanticipated outcomes.

Slowly, these leaders infused the culture with the pre-eminent values of integrity and truth-telling. As these ideas took hold, along with collaboration rather than competition, evolution of our culture—what we think of as maturation, was effortless. The almost magical joys of aesthetic and ascetic personal development, learning, and teaching, together with reverence for individual spirituality prevailed. The result was a drastic reduction in conflict, internal stress, hatred, envy, and stunted emotional growth. This stress reduction combined with advances in science made medical costs negligible as well as the costs of litigation, crime control, and military establishments. Then as you might surmise, enlightened voters and consumers rapidly brought about sensible community development, sharp declines in ethnic and religious conflicts, competent governance, and honest, accurate reporting. Many of the intractable issues presently damaging your so-called civilization became almost effortlessly self-healing for us. The few antisocial or underdeveloped individuals were easily rehabilitated by caring communities.

Is that all it took—integrity and truth-telling?

Of course not. However, one surprise was that once integrity, honesty, and goodwill took hold, it was like removal of a log jam; lots of good things followed almost effortlessly.

Like what?

Our democracy quickly became effective and durable. Mass-media journalism had to become truthful and by our interpretations of truth and integrity, that also meant complete and unbiased. This reduced the entertainment and reassurance value of news broadcasts, but it certainly raised the understanding and par-

ticipation of voters. Coming to recognize the power for good or evil of voting, citizens voted to require qualifying tests to license all voters and penalizing non-voters.

It sounds ideal, like Nirvana.

I thought so too, until meeting you. Now I'm not quite so sure.

What do you mean by that?

Let me finish summarizing our planet's transition. As I mentioned, our pervasive integrity and truth-telling almost instantly upgraded our governance, most particularly our modes of leadership selection. At critical moments in transitioning, we were blessed with inspired, specially trained leaders who were able to anticipate the future sufficiently to advance the foundation of true civilization. The legal systems, S&T policies, tax structures, and political processes were in place when needed. Occasionally, episodes of "terrorism" induced fear and further expanded compliance with the public and leadership's realistic, enlightened responses. A major consequence was the formation of a limited form of world government.

I'm afraid that would be a very gradual, tortuous process for us here.

You may be right. There was a very bad period for us, as I mentioned earlier, which may also be inevitable in your own transitioning. Our democracy, akin to your current one, was flawed here and there, but basically worked. Our electorate did control the choice of leaders which they adjusted according to approval or disapproval of what was done. But like you, we entered a period where the voters, leaders, and systems just weren't good enough in their understanding, competencies, and response times. The consequent chaos was painful, but apparently the only way for us to initiate our enlightenment revolution. In the case of this planet, I suspect that the only way to avoid the same painful, wasteful disruption requires an enlightenment revolution that can proceed faster than the forces of conventional revolution; some of which, incidentally, you incorrectly classify as terrorism.

It sounds grim ... too grim. You seem upbeat about it. Is it that you feel detached?

Regardless of how I feel, let me mention the obvious. It doesn't seem easy to cross a threshold when the door is closed. I'm just pointing out that your planet is at thresholds with doors that can easily be opened. It's not at all like standing at the edge of a deep chasm, although I admit you can't see the difference when the doors are closed.

I appreciate the metaphor. Except that we Earthlings often use metaphors to avoid answering a question. I'm feeling very uneasy at this moment. Please answer me. Do you feel detached?

Of course not, certainly not on a personal level. How could you even ask that? There isn't time for a lengthy discussion of this now. But I must tell you that despite my fantasies, the reality is that I must return home promptly. And I'm eager to do so.

Your ability to casually hurt me remains intact. You're leaving me ... us ... just like that? What about our unfinished work? What about your comment about your planet not quite being the same Nirvana since meeting me? I don't get it at all!

You may feel less hurt if you let me finish. Regarding our interaction, you have affected me profoundly at a personal level. The intensity of our interaction is unknown on my planet. I'm beginning to believe that we may have gradually and inadvertently accepted rather diluted modes of interpersonal relations as the price of harmony, tranquility and stability. If so, I now suspect that in that process we've lost dynamism, vibrancy, creativity, and innovation. If I correctly understand how to apply your systems analysis, this leaves us vulnerable to sudden external changes and limits our capacity to enjoy and contribute to each other internally. All of which leaves me convinced that contrary to what I'd grown up believing, my planet is not Nirvana. It has little joy, and no unfettered spirit. I'm even concerned that our much touted security and stability may be an illusion of the moment.

I feel badly for you. You were so comfortable and self-confident when we met. Have I done this to you?

No, no. Of course not. You've described the life cycle of engineering systems as a series of phases. At home we look at life similarly. You've helped me as I transition to the next phase and it is frightening, depressing and exhilarating all intermixed. The same thing must happen here too and often.

That sounds right. In fact what you describe reminds me of how, on a smaller scale, my children left their comfortable, secure home for college. Your actual situation is far more serious of course. What can you do about it?

I'm not sure. I've already started by writing a concerto, atonal, a passionate work with a radically different structure from the norm—our norm. I'll send you a download if I can. It will offend and threaten, attracting attention from a few critics who are well connected in our sociopolitical networks. That will start some discourse which I suspect will propagate widely. I'm also thinking of becoming a mother, the "old fashioned" way. That may cause more excitement than my concerto. May we continue tomorrow?

Of course; same time.

Session 37

OK, what about our unfinished work?

I hope you never believed that our work could ever be finished. Even for an engineer.... ☺

Touché. Let's at least summarize where we think we are at this point.

Good idea.

OK. Let me ask the first critical question. What's our present overall situation as you see it?

That's easy, albeit ominous. You have some very real existential threats:

- *There is the potential for major disorder, particularly the loss of life together with loss of the economic, sociopolitical, and cultural advances within your civilization. Plus, I haven't yet mentioned the probable destruction of vital resources and severe degradation of a sustainable ecology. This is serious stuff; I've seen the pattern too often elsewhere to be mistaken.*

- *The problems primarily derive from indiscriminant proliferation of weapons, S&T, information, and drugs. This combination overloads your rather primitive health, education, and welfare systems, and is exacerbated by limitations of your economic, sociopolitical, and cultural systems. This mindless proliferation is simply indigestible.*

- *Stakeholders who control and manage organizations are unwilling to share power, wealth, or access. To maintain constituents' loyalty and their own self-respect while in denial, they become myopic, even dishonest with themselves and deceptive with others. In confronting opponents they will lie or obfuscate, then resort to threats and suppression—behaviors that are inflammatory and counterproductive.*

- *Governmental institutions and their leadership's policies and strategies are dangerously anachronistic with capricious economic policies. Vital sources of information, especially the mass-media, unscrupulously pursue market share, bombarding audiences with entertainment and fear-reassurances.*

Offsetting these threats you have opportunities:

- *Globalization provides proximity in geography, information, and culture. If your daughter finds her mate from another culture and locale, you will want to help him be healthy, employed, and psychologically mature. He and his family will want her to be intellectually, culturally, and emotionally mature. Their children will have a more enlightened world view; such melting-pot mechanisms and incentives abound.*

- *The earth has a surplus of fallow or misdirected resources and technologies; offering new opportunities and efficiencies in information technologies and nano sciences, in health, conflict management, and much else.*

So in confronting these threats and opportunities what do you see as the most important challenges to be addressed?

Excellent and totally predictable question, my engineer and erstwhile lover. The overarching challenge I see is to facilitate the rapid evolution of the structures and mechanisms of governance to assure the emergence of policies and leaders who are competent and favorably disposed to address these challenges:

- *Controlling WMD and potential perpetrators of terror, including individuals, independent or networked cells, and governments. This must be done but in such a manner as to preserve, even enhance, the several civilizations and cultures in jeopardy.*

- *Modernizing weapons and their usage; developing devices and methods that contain rather than maim or inflame. Weapons that immobilize rather than destroy lives and property create fewer new enemies and post-hostility burdens for the victor.*

- *Developing devices that:*

  - *detect the locations and intentions of perpetrators;*

  - *provide for harmless but effective interrogations, rehabilitation and/or incarceration; and*

  - *rapidly assess damage and the source of attacks.*

- *Accelerating enlightened development within the five E's: Economics, Education, Employment, Environment, and Energy.*

- *Expanding personal, family, and community development.*

- *Installing a dynamic jurisprudence and justice system that pragmatically balances external challenges to society versus individuals' rights and freedoms.*

- *Fostering and safeguarding morality, aesthetic and cultural values.*

Can you delineate programs for addressing these challenges?

Isn't that a bit much to expect from an extraterrestrial musicologist? About all that I can do is speculate about enabling objectives that your programs might address such as:

- *Creating a Global Federation or irrevocable alliances focused on WMD control and initiatives for economic and sociopolitical resources and cultural development.*

- *Fostering enlightened, equitable economic systems.*

- *Establishing equitable sociopolitical constructs with justice and individual rights in balance.*

- *Developing long-range but self-sustaining S&T policies that emphasize energy needs, environment, health care, and education.*

- *Promoting integrity, especially in politics, law, commerce, media, education, and religion.*

- *Modernizing election processes to ensure financial transparency, honest media content, accurate vote counting, and testing to qualify candidates and voters.*

So how do we bring about implementation?

Ah, the key question of course! You've been around here longer than I have. What are your thoughts?

I can only recite some general insights, maybe guidelines from lessons learned in my work:

- Change is more attainable if there are at least some common goals, understandings, and mutual trust or obligations among stakeholders. This is obvious, but often difficult to attain.

- Institutional blockages or "organizational arthritis" is common and may have many causes, including comfort with the traditional operational modes, leadership conflicts, and limited influence over external stakeholders and events. The obvious importance of knowing the causes before applying remedies is often ignored.

- In addition, conceptual and behavioral blockages must also be understood and overcome, such as attitudes and habits, risk-reward estimates, incomplete information dissemination, interpretation, and utilization.

- Mistaken perceptions thrive regarding stakeholders' identity and propensities, the consequences of resource allocations, of personnel and organizational capabilities. Even when perceptions happen to be correct, the future is dynamic and "non-linear," departing suddenly from the past at critical moments.

I'd add one more to your list: compatibility with the pace and magnitude of external events. On our planet, when the external environment was moving slowly, our efforts at accommodations—especially at enlightened democracy backed by supportive S&T, paid off. At other times, a fast-moving, large-scale conflict would spawn an autocratic military, economic, and/or religion-based empire.

So what initiatives make sense for us? If you and I could gather the world leaders together and brief them in these broad-brush strokes on the trouble we're in, citing strategic objectives we've prioritized which they should implement, what would happen?

Well, judging from your excellent compilation of barriers to change, I'd guess that they would forge a resolution with sufficient euphemisms and wiggle room, release it to the media, and then head off to their private jets for a relaxing flight home.

Well, that's a very cute response, but what should we try to do, given our limited access to the basic change mechanisms, resources, and to knowing the unknowable future??

I suggest that we both think things over and reconvene at our regular time tomorrow. OK?

Done.

SESSION 38

So, have you had any inspiring thoughts in the last twenty-four hours? Is there anything from your experience or analyses to suggest?

I've had lots of ideas, the best of which is to organize some field trip research. I've concluded that you and I need more information as to how other cultures are doing. I can suggest an island in the South Pacific which has great snorkeling and diving. I make an excellent rum mai tai.

Please be serious. We don't have much more time. My suggestion is for you to form an organization; call it SOSA.

It sounds like a detergent. What is it? And what do you mean, "We don't have much more time?"

SOSA stands for the Seeds of Survival Association. The name isn't important. SOSA would campaign to help initiate:

- *Universal public service conscription;*

- *S&T priorities in energy, health, education, food, and media;*

- *Modernized processes of leadership selection and governance; and*

- *Universal mechanisms for providing current, unbiased, relevant education and information.*

I've sketched out a plan of action for you.

NOTES: SOSA will become a very broad-based membership organization. You will first assemble a small team of founders: investors, retired executives, military leaders, and outstanding academicians with "think-tank" and foundation support. This group would then formulate a comprehensively designed program plan, which would include the immediate design and implementation of a specialized blog. I'd expect this blog to include a "Sesame Street" for grownups; to embody entertainment, consumer reports, and easy-access networking with other blogs, as well as annotated links to eBay, Google, Yahoo, and other sources of information. It would also feature impeccably neutral, 24/7 current events with various intelligent interpretations. If you get it right, it could become very powerful. Just stand aside and watch it evolve.

How quickly could it grow?

If, for example, an average of one active member per month could be recruited and mentored, and then that member does the same, more than 100 million members could belong within two years. It might take four years if the average was only one new active recruit every two months.

The logistics of a 100 million-member grass roots organization could be challenging. How might that work?

Certainly without lots of hierarchical, micro-managing. And 100 million is a number intended to demonstrate the possibilities. One primary requirement would be to keep it legal, transparent, and non-threatening to non-participants, especially to pre-existing institutions that claim to be doing pieces of the same kind of work.

Each individual joining SOSA would pledge to conduct the following activities:

• *<u>Never lie</u>. Reserve the right to silence, but tell the truth when communicating;*

• *<u>Save at least one life per year anonymously</u>, acting individually or in group;*

• *<u>Recruit and mentor at least one member per month</u>;*

• *Sharpen each member's nonverbal <u>communication and perception skills</u> in an annual training activity;*

• *Design and pursue initiatives that contribute to <u>self-awareness and self-actualization</u>, including the setting of goals and metrics with a partner for mutual support and assessment; and*

• *Contribute to helping involvement in multiple institutions, including the <u>macro-family concept</u>.*

The political leaders, the military and other government agencies, once they recognize how SOSA helps their respective objectives; they will gradually become supportive. Suppose, for example, that half the membership pledges to watch their own neighborhoods and report any imminent acts of terrorism, drug abuse, or human rights violations. Such a sizeable membership could matter. As with issues of the physical environment, an ecology-of-civilization movement would soon capture the attention of the private sector and encourage participation, either for new products and services or for concern over image to investors, employees, regulators, and customers.

The logic of this seems unassailable. As outlined, it is not a highly structured program at this stage, mainly because it is inherently self-structuring. Its very nature requires that it be somewhat fluid and restructured by the membership as it evolves.

> *The first challenge is to convey the importance of imminent threats together with the feasibility of remedial opportunities.*
>
> *The second challenge is to convince individuals that their concerted action can successfully produce the remedies.*
>
> *The third challenge is to motivate and win individuals' commitment to action.*
>
> *The fourth challenge is to convince and motivate key stakeholders to share their particular resources, authority, culture, and knowledge.*

Unfortunately, after working so hard to acquire and retain these treasures, most stakeholders will probably continue resisting actively or passively, as necessary, to retain them. Only after seeing and/or causing many deaths from this steadfast retention of their "treasure" did our key stakeholders understand that it was in their own self-interest to "let go." I hope Earthlings will be different, but I see little cause for optimism at this stage.

Is SOSA the only way to go?

No, of course not. I think it's a viable example that may or may not work, depending on circumstances and timing. But the underlying thinking could be important to designing and implementing any SOSA-type initiatives.

Why not a POSA, that is, "Plants" rather than "Seeds?" Can't we save precious time and minimize startup mistakes by resorting to existing organizations?

Excellent question! I'm really going to miss you ... us. Look, I presume you mean that "plants" are your existing entities that have organizational structure and global reach, resources, and the poten-

tial insight, self-interest, and commitment to perform what's needed. So what kind of entities might qualify?

I see what you're getting at. I think of governments, think-tanks, and foundations, organized religions, military establishments, and industries. They would have the necessary resources, organization, and outreach. But governments and religions are too often locked into their traditions and leadership rigidities. Think-tanks typically lack open advocacy, organizational, and networking strengths. Pre-existing foundations have pre-existing agendas and cultures. That leaves military and industry entities, both of which hate conflict but enjoy competition—some of them might be hosts for grafting "slips" from SOSA seedlings. We need to get more explicit regarding implementation incentives, that is, the carrots and sticks. Maybe that's for the founding task force to focus on. Are you confident? Can we make this happen?

I think so. You do need the carrots and sticks as well as widespread recognition as to which is which. You need smart leaders and followers who are courageous enough to acknowledge their realities. You can expect that many people, ranging from thoughtless misers to thoughtful conservatives, will feel threatened and intervene whenever possible. Even if the preliminary and detailed systems designs of SOSA are successful, continuous change will be necessary and difficult. Uncontrollable, unpredictable circumstances may prove disastrous. If SOSA's majority is blinded or arrogant from some initial successes, or if growth causes it to become insensitive to small regional and cultural differences, it will fail or become irrelevant. If you think of it as an incubating process rather than an institution, it may work better.

Have you suggested this or seen it work with other planets?

No. I would not even suggest any of this except for the fact that I find Earthlings and this planet resource-rich, innovative, spiritual, and beautiful. Having learned about, and having become deeply respectful of, these attributes convinces me that you can and must survive and succeed. We need more of you gifted people and planets in our cosmos.

That's delightful to hear. Less delightful was your comment that our time is limited. Did you mean what I think you meant? I don't want you to leave—certainly not yet. You must know that I want you to stay here with me forever. I plead with you to stay. But at the same time, believing as you do that my planet is possibly doomed and certainly in for an abominable decade or two, part of me insists that you not stay here despite knowing how much I will miss you—us!

Me too—more than I know how to communicate. The reality is, I'm grateful to have known you. You have given me and perhaps my planet far more than I've given you. And you must know that whatever insights and wisdom I could possibly convey to you, you are now your own. I'll try to e-mail from time to time—if you'll let me get past your spam filters. ☺

Wait! Not yet! I need to be sure that we're making the right decisions and for the right reasons.

My sweet and charming engineer. If it's the right decision, what difference do the reasons … never mind. All right, I know how this will end but let's go through the process, "systematically." Will you please come home with me? Why do I ask? My first, most elemental reason is simply wanting to save you. I don't want anyone I care about to stay in this dangerous place. So please come home with me where you'll be safe!

Next, I want you to come home with me because I've never felt so euphoric and so immersed in a relationship; selfishly, I don't want to give you up. And finally, from this euphoria, I feel a powerful urge to share. I want to teach ... no, I want to share with my planet and perhaps my future children what I've discovered here with us. Which is?

How can I express it? I've been a supportive, well-adjusted product of a planet that values, and indeed insists on, collaboration rather than competition, reality rather than fantasy, terrorism protection by means of surveillance and macro-family membership rather than privacy. We depend on artificial sensory gratification from an imbedded chip rather than experiential personal effort. We have impersonal state-run procreation and macro-family imperatives. All of these tools and more assure stability and creature comfort of our species and protection of the ecology.

But through our all-too-brief encounter I've come to see my planet as a macro-womb. My people have created a hyper-stable planet, so stable and orderly, in fact, that intense joy, challenge, and development of the human spirit have been subordinated. Conveying this insight to my people is an obligation that unfortunately transcends your most tempting invitation to stay here with you. Hopefully I'll find others at home ready to move on, to engage the challenges essential to maturation and spiritual self-realization. I'd rather be here with you. This planet, while it lasts, offers excitement and self-actualization opportunities. But that's also why, paradoxically, I absolutely most go home. I'm finding it difficult to ... please, you talk.

Know that I want to spend my life with you, even when you tease me about wanting reasons. That's probably my engineering reflex. But remember, if I don't like how my system design is evolving, I'll automatically re-examine the details in search of a happier outcome. Or maybe I'm just sad and frustrated, and don't want to look at the insurmountable dichotomy of this relationship. Out of our love, I intensely want to be wherever you are, but I also intensely want to do anything I can to support harmony and growth in your life and work. I may finally have learned that not all dichotomies can be resolved. I'm sure you understand that I must stay here and work to save this planet, using what I have learned from you as my guide.

Of course I understand, partly because we both feel the same responsibility to use the insights we have gained for more than ourselves. There's no assurance that I'll be successful, but I must try, too. Do you believe you can make a difference?

Truthfully, I don't. But I have to try.

Me too. And if unsuccessful ... well, please keep your e-mail account active ☹

E P I L O G U E

—————————— ▼ ——————————

"It's been a year and you still haven't upgraded your firewall! And you've been too busy to shut down our chat room? ☺
You're back!! I can't believe it! No, I didn't … I couldn't shut it down. Where are you? Can we get together? What have you been doing? Tell me everything.
I will, but you first. How are your goldfish? Have you remarried? Earth's civilization seems largely intact—do you deserve credit for that?
You're back—wonderful! OK, the goldfish moved to a "higher level of aggregation;" a flaw in their food-dispenser mechanism while I was on a ski trip. My other suit is back from the cleaners, and on dates, I'm now able to avoid thinking about you after only two or three martinis. Of greater interest, I've assembled a small task force which has designed and test-marketed our SOSA program. We're about ready to launch and I'd love for you to be part of it—and of me. Of course, if you're otherwise encumbered—your turn.
My turn. Well, it's been quite a year. I was greeted with relief and warmth from my close circle of people. I tried, but there was no traction in relating to them or others individually. Our equivalent

of your two-or-three martini mechanism worked for me, too, but seemed pointless. I'd gone home thinking about having a child, but once there, I realized that for me, it would have to evolve from a committed, caring relationship. I'm afraid that our collaboration somehow "raised the bar" for me.

Besides, I needed to complete my concerto, which took time and more emotional energy than I'd expected. It received mixed reviews, as did my efforts to entice my "circle" to venture forth into new and possibly uncomfortable adventures, both intellectually and politically. I did manage to get some things going, but it's hard when people are so self-satisfied. I'd like your perspective on all of that and some related issues. So yes, let's get together. Is our favorite restaurant available?

Great! I'll make a reservation for tonight. Meanwhile, help me catch up. Have you a key insight or "lesson learned" from this past year you'd like me to be thinking about?

Let's see … yes, OK. I think my bumper sticker might read something like, "Nirvana is overrated." Frankly, going home from here to "perfection" was crazy for me. Thanks to you and this place, I now need to live at some level of tension, uncertainty, and challenge.

Thanks, I think. Well, to reciprocate, my bumper sticker might read, "Survival is Overrated." I came to realize during this drab year without you that while we'd been working together, devoting our efforts entirely to global survival, that worked beautifully because our relationship had love, excitement, discovery, that, and we were alive! But this past year, just focusing on survival, well … it reminds me of the doctor's comment to his patient: "You're telling me that you've given up wind-surfing, alcohol, red meat, and women in order to live longer—why would you want to?"

I'm looking forward to our dinner—and living life.